WAYNE STINNETT

MERCILESS CHARITY

A CHARITY STYLES NOVEL

Caribbean Thriller Series
Volume 1

D1571743

2015

Published by DOWN ISLAND PRESS, 2015
Travelers Rest, SC
Copyright © 2015 by Wayne Stinnett

Library of Congress cataloging-in-publication Data
Stinnett, Wayne
Merciless Charity/Wayne Stinnett
p. cm. - (A Charity Styles novel)
ISBN-13: 978-0692548806 (Down Island Press)
ISBN-10: 0692548807

Graphics by Tim Ebaugh Photography and Design
Edited by Clio Editing Services
Proofreading by Donna Rich
Interior Design by Write.Dream.Repeat. Book Design

Most of the locations herein are also fictional, or are used fictitiously. However, I took great pains to depict the location and description of the many well-known islands, locales, beaches, reefs, bars, and restaurants in the Keys, to the best of my ability.

FOREWORD

I'd like to thank the many people who encouraged me to branch out and start this new series. Writing from a woman's point of view, even in third person, wasn't the easiest thing for me. As always, my biggest fan and best critic has been my wife. Without her encouragement, I would have given up after the first book.

A special debt of gratitude is owed to the many writers and writing professionals of Author's Corner, for all the great ideas, encouragement, and counsel.

Thanks also to beta readers Alan Fader, Marc Lowe, David Parsons, Jeanne Gelbert, Dana Vihlen, Ted Nulty, Debbie Kocol, and Tom Crisp. Your input has been extremely valuable in making this book better than it was.

DEDICATION

To my stepdaughter and her husband, Nikki and Jason Ruhf. The support and guidance you've provided has been worth far more than I can ever put into words.

"It is better to die on your feet than to live on your knees."
- **Emiliano Zapata**, 1911

If you'd like to receive my twice a month newsletter for specials, book recommendations, and updates on coming books, please sign up on my website:

WWW.WAYNESTINNETT.COM

THE CHARITY STYLES CARIBBEAN THRILLER SERIES

Merciless Charity
Ruthless Charity (Summer, 2016)
Heartless Charity (Winter, 2017)

THE JESSE MCDERMITT CARIBBEAN ADVENTURE SERIES

Fallen Out
Fallen Palm
Fallen Hunter
Fallen Pride
Fallen Mangrove
Fallen King
Fallen Honor
Fallen Tide
Fallen Angel
Fallen Hero (Fall, 2016)

The Gaspar's Revenge Ship's Store is now open. There you can purchase all kinds of swag related to my books.
WWW.GASPARS-REVENGE.COM

MERCILESS
CHARITY

CHAPTER ONE:

At first glance, the man appeared youthful, though he was in his fifties. His dark hair, trimmed unfashionably short, was just starting to turn gray around the temples. On closer inspection under the flickering firelight, creases could be seen at the corners of his gray-blue eyes.

He sat at a large outdoor table with a younger blond woman, their faces lit only by the Tiki torches around the table. The tiny island they were on, miles from anywhere, was idyllic, and under other circumstances the woman might find the scene romantic.

"This is the only way this can work," he told her, sliding a file folder across the table.

The woman sitting across from him was attractive. He'd noted this early on, with some foreshadowing sadness. She was in her late twenties, slim, with broader shoulders than most women, the result of having been an Olympic swimmer seven years earlier. She wore her hair at a medium length, just below her shoulders. Her complexion was flawless, deeply tanned as a result of having grown up in Southern California and spending a lot of her time outdoors.

The blonde looked at the file and gave it only a moment's thought before picking it up and folding it into the inside pocket of her vest. She'd read the details later, when she was alone.

Right now they had a more pressing concern: protecting one of their own people and his family. She'd arrived with four others, helicoptering to this tiny outlying island in the Florida Keys backcountry. An imminent threat had been received, and the target of that threat was the man who owned the island and occasionally provided transportation for their clandestine group.

The man across from her was Associate Deputy Director Travis Stockwell, head of the Caribbean Counterterrorism Command and her boss's boss. They were on the island as part of a protection force, whether the target liked it or not.

The blonde was the helicopter pilot and martial arts instructor for the group, comprised of former military special operators and other high-speed, low-drag law enforcement and intelligence assets. Charity Styles was no stranger to situations like this.

Approaching the table was the man she had come to help protect. Charity also found him attractive, though he too was quite a few years older than she was. Over six feet tall, lithe and powerfully built, Jesse McDermitt probably didn't need anyone protecting him from a Miami street gang, but the group numbered in the hundreds and was known to be ruthless.

Stockwell looked up and spoke to McDermitt as he approached the table. "When the deputy brings your daughter home, it would probably be wise for him to stay here." McDermitt's daughter, Kim, had left the island earlier in the evening to go on a dinner date with a local Monroe deputy sheriff.

"Yeah, I was gonna suggest that," McDermitt agreed. "I know he knows his way around the water down near the bigger islands, but it's real easy to get lost up here if you don't know the way really well."

McDermitt was a retired Marine sniper. Charity had thought him to be some sort of a hermit upon meeting him for the first time a year earlier. He operated a part-time charter service for divers and fishermen, but spent most of his days alone on this island. Over the past year, he'd changed. After inheriting a good bit of money from his late wife's estate last year and then finding a valuable Spanish treasure six months ago, he'd turned his little island into a staging area for the group's missions.

They were all a part of a clandestine counterterrorism team under the direct control of Stockwell's boss, the Secretary of Homeland Security.

A month after the terrorist attacks of September 11th, Charity had applied to and been accepted by the Army's Officer Candidate School. Her father, a Vietnam veteran, had been a crop duster, and had taught his young daughter to fly.

Six months later, while flying a medevac chopper, Charity had been shot down in the district of Dai Chopan in Zabul Province, Afghanistan. She had been injured, but managed to evade the enemy for several hours. Eventually she had been captured by the Taliban fighters.

She'd been raped and sodomized twenty-nine times over the following days, until Coalition Forces had mounted a raid in the desolate terrain. She'd been able to kill her one guard in the confusion and make her escape.

After that, Charity had spent several months in rehab, trying to cope with what had happened during her captivity. In the end, she'd been quietly mustered out with a medical discharge.

A year ago, after more than three years as a martial arts instructor for Miami-Dade police, Charity had been invited to join a new counterterrorism team based out of nearby Homestead Air Reserve base. She'd jumped at the chance. Her experiences at the hands of her captors had left a mark, but Charity had learned to turn that part of her brain on and off at will. Unleashing that part of her mind where the demons dwelled made her very dangerous, a fact which hadn't gone unnoticed.

Charity had helped McDermitt find the treasure along with several others he'd invited. She was due a share of it, which could set her up for life. If she wanted that kind of boring life.

McDermitt had originally been contracted to covertly transport personnel and equipment to hot spots around South Florida and the Caribbean in his charter boat. Up until now, Charity's position on the team had been a bit less covert. The CCC was a badged agency under Homeland Security, and the group of operatives, while comprised of mostly military people, were badged agents much like the FBI or DEA. Covert, but not as covert as McDermitt. He was a freelancer and didn't carry a badge. Once Charity put the file folder from Stockwell in her pocket, she became more covert. Only Stockwell, the secretary, and the president would know her new assignment.

Stockwell had approached Charity several months earlier with a proposition—one that came directly from the DHS secretary and ostensibly had the approval of the president as well. Stockwell had told her then that if she accepted the proposal, she'd operate strictly under his control, with plausible deniability for both the president and secretary.

The proposal was simple. Stockwell would be seen as retiring from public service and would be replaced by McDermitt. From time to time, a courier would deliver a physical file to Stockwell, who would then fly to Charity's location and hand-deliver it.

Charity's new job would be a lot more difficult and dangerous than her old one. Having no family and no close friends to speak of, she was the ideal candidate. At a time of her choosing, she would *steal* the unmarked helicopter she was currently piloting and disappear into thin air. That was the cover story, and only Stockwell and McDermitt would know the real story. When she reappeared somewhere in the Caribbean, someone would die.

"That's what I was thinking," Stockwell said to McDermitt. "If he ran across a boatful of Haitians, a fast exit wouldn't be a good idea. Do you know when they'll be back?"

"No later than twenty-one hundred," McDermitt replied.

Nodding to the director and rising from the table, Charity said, "I'm going to get some rest." With another nod to McDermitt, she left them there. No doubt the director would speak to McDermitt soon about taking over his position as the head of the two counterterrorism teams. At least then he would know what was about to happen. The others on the team would be left to believe a fabricated story.

Charity walked toward the bunkhouse in the dim light from the torches and campfires. McDermitt had originally built it and another just like it to house their team. The one on the west side had been converted so that half of it was a communications center and housing for the women on the team. It was also where McDermitt's daughter was staying, since the main house only had one bedroom.

Earlier in the evening, the team's communications and electronics specialist had arrived, and now she was busy setting up her equipment. Chyrel Koshinski was a small woman and likable, but Charity maintained only a cool working relationship with her, as well as with the other team members.

As she walked past, the two women exchanged greetings, and Charity reclined on the far bunk to look at the file Stockwell had just given her. Facing Chyrel, so the contents of the file couldn't be viewed, she removed it from her vest pocket and opened it. She was sure the other woman wouldn't ask, and equally sure that if she saw anything, she'd keep it to herself. Chyrel had come to the CCC team from an organization known for keeping secrets. She was a former CIA computer analyst.

The first page of the file was the typical physical description, along with two photographs. In the first, the target appeared to be in custody. Though wearing a full beard, he had closely cropped hair and wore an orange jumpsuit. She confirmed his identity on the next page.

Captured in the Arma Mountains in Afghanistan during Operation Anaconda in March of 2002, Hussein Seif al Din Asfour had been twenty-three when captured as a Taliban fighter. He had been sent to the detention facility in Guantanamo Bay and detained there until 2004, when he was transferred into Uruguayan custody. He'd escaped and left the country less than a year later.

The second photo was obviously taken at long range with a surveillance camera. However, the image quality was very good and, looking from one photo to the other, Charity could easily tell they were of the same man. She read further in the file.

After his escape, al Din Asfour had returned to Afghanistan, where he had disappeared in the ranks of the Taliban for nearly a year. The later photograph was taken just two months ago, in the Mexican state of Veracruz. It'd been reported that a Hezbollah training camp had been established deep in the remote forest-covered southern slope of the massive San Martin Tuxtla volcano.

As she read, Charity became tired, her eyes slowly closing. Her chin dropped, but a sound jolted her awake. Looking over the file, she saw that Chyrel was slumped back in her chair. Realizing that something was terribly wrong, Charity put the file back into her vest pocket before rising from the bunk. She made it halfway to her feet, before her legs simply stopped working and she collapsed back on the bunk.

CHAPTER TWO:

S lowly, the sun disappeared behind the distant mountain peaks, leaving the high, wispy clouds bathed in a pale orange-and-pink afterglow.

Awad Qureshi finished his evening prayer and rolled up his prayer mat. From his vantage point on the north rim of a long-dormant volcano, Awad had a commanding view of the surrounding terrain and its approaches. His relief would be coming up the trail out of the forest soon, and he was hungry.

He'd only arrived at this desolate location two weeks earlier. Each of the fifteen men in the group had arrived separately over the course of several days, making their way in whatever fashion they could. Awad had come by way of a small freighter to a port just sixty kilometers northwest of where the group was now camped.

Being fluent in both Spanish and English, he had it easier than most of his companions and was able to get a ride with a farmer to within fifteen kilometers of the volcano.

The group of men had been instructed to go by foot the last fifteen kilometers, and though the last leg of his journey had been very difficult, the terrain wasn't all that different than his homeland. The last of the group had arrived a week ago, and training had begun the following day.

At all times, one of the group was on this high escarpment, three hundred feet above the valley below. This high rim was above the surrounding trees, and when it was clear, Awad could see the distant ocean, twenty kilometers to the north, stretching away diagonally to the east as the shoreline curved around the outflow from a long-ago eruption.

Down in the valley below, actually the volcano's crater, gunfire erupted sporadically. Surrounded by the high rim of the volcanic basin, the sound was shielded from anyone near the base of the great mountain. The kilometer-wide crater was the perfect training site.

The group's actual camp was to the south, down the treacherous and densely forested escarpment. Occasionally, tourists were known to hike the trails on the northern and eastern slopes, which were much easier to traverse and provided spectacular views. The western slope was popular with rock climbers, as it had many canyons cut deep into the side of the mountain. It was also closer to the only highway in the area. But the southern slope was heavily forested, a deep jungle that rose forty feet to a canopy of leaves that all but blocked out the sunlight. After a week of traipsing back and forth on the game trail several times a day, the men in the group no longer even needed a light at night.

Fortunately, tourists and rock climbers were uncommon this time of year, due to the oppressive heat. Lookouts rarely reported a truck or car going by on the highway below. There was little chance their camp would be discovered, and they trained only in the rocky confines of the crater, where the terrain was at least level.

Movement caught Awad's eye from the trail below. He picked up his binoculars and held them to his eyes. It was his relief, bringing his evening meal. All but the group's leader shared the responsibility of standing lookout on the barren rocks above the valley.

Each man stood watch for only two hours at a time. With fourteen sharing this duty, always relieving and being relieved by the same person, Awad's assigned time was several hours later every day.

Reaching the lookout spot at the summit, Faud Assaf sat down across from Awad and said, "As-salamu alaykum."

"Wa-Alaikum-Salaam," Awad replied. "What do we have for dinner?"

"You are always hungry, my friend," Faud replied. "I fear you may have a tapeworm in your stomach."

Faud passed a small covered bowl to Awad. "Majdi killed one of the small deer this afternoon."

Awad removed the earthen lid from the bowl and set it aside. Using his fingers, he quickly devoured the spicy stew, licking his fingers clean.

"As always," Awad said, wiping his mouth on the sleeve of his shirt, "there is nothing of significance to report.

Two cars went by on the highway, but neither of them stopped."

"Hussein wishes to see you upon your return. He has more questions for you on American culture."

Rising, Awad picked up his rifle, stowed the empty bowl in his pack and started down the steep cliff to the trail that would lead him to the training area. He would meet with the leader and then retire to the camp to rest before the morning training session.

It was fully dark when Awad arrived at the valley floor. The others had already ended their training and were nowhere to be found. It took another thirty minutes to hike down the southern slope to the camp. Though the sky was clear and a bright moon was overhead, it provided little light to guide his way.

Reaching the camp, he went directly to the leader's tent, tapped on the front support post and waited. The flap was pulled back and the group's leader, Hussein Seif al Din Asfour, said, "*It-fad-dal*, Awad. *As-salamu alaykum*."

"*Wa-Alaikum-Salaam*, Hussein. Faud said you wished to see me."

Awad entered the tent and waited until the group leader sat on the bare dirt floor and motioned for him to sit also.

"How long did you stay in America?" Hussein asked.

"Three years."

"You learned much in those three years at the American university."

Awad nodded. "At the university, yes. But I learned much more outside the classroom."

"We will move against the infidels in two weeks."

"That soon?" Awad asked. The group had only been to-gether for a short time, and it seemed premature.

"Yes, I understand it seems a short period. Howev-er, our target is an easy one, an event that only happens once every year. You are second in command and it is time you know what that target is."

"Allah willing, I will martyr myself in glory."

Hussein reached behind him and picked up a small hookah. Awad was uncomfortable with the use of opi-um, particularly by someone in power, but he dared not say anything.

"Do you know the city of San Antonio, in Texas?"

"I know of it," Awad replied. "I have never been there." This seemed to trouble Hussein, so Awad continued, "America is a very large country with many thousands of cities. Even Americans who travel often will never see them all."

"There is a place in this city. A place called River Walk. At this place every year, they celebrate their military's conquest over Allah's people and drink alcohol."

"I have heard of this," Awad said. "It is televised live."

Hussein's mouth curled into a sadistic smile. "That is the main reason I chose it."

Hussein lit the hookah and inhaled deeply. "There are many shops and restaurants along this River Walk, and tour boats that carry dozens of people along its length. We will separate into three groups on three of these boats. When the time is right, we will kill the infidels on the boats and as many as we can on this River Walk. You will lead the first boat, I will lead the second and Majdi will lead the third."

"It is many kilometers to this city," Awad said, "with many dangers along the way, just to get to the American border."

Hussein nodded. "This is another reason why we will go in three groups. Majdi has been living in America for several years and speaks both English and Spanish. I learned English, as well as Spanish, while I was being held at the American prison, and you are fluent in both languages as well. Once across the border, we will rent separate vehicles in McAllen for the journey to San Antonio."

Awad thought for a moment. Hussein had been a captive of the Americans for some time, held at their prison in Cuba. The Spanish he had learned there was very different from that of the Mexican peasants here. But Hussein had a reputation for being quick to fly off the handle, so Awad was hesitant to point this out. Perhaps anyone he came into contact with would think him a visitor from another Central or South American country.

"How do we get from here to the border?"

"A drug cartel, one of the most powerful in Mexico, will provide a truck to transport all of us to Reynosa, across the border from McAllen, in two weeks' time. In Reynosa, we will be provided with paperwork that will allow us to cross the border without issue, mixed in with a large group of workers. Go now. Get rested. We have much preparation over the next two weeks."

Without another word, Awad rose and left the leader's tent. Outside, he stood silently in the darkness until his eyesight adjusted and then made his way to his own tent.

CHAPTER THREE:

Shaking her head groggily, Charity looked around the room. Chyrel was still slumped back in her chair, but something was different. Her hair. It hadn't been falling down the back of the chair a moment ago.

Gingerly, her head throbbing, Charity moved her long legs, spreading her feet further apart for better balance. She slowly stood up as Chyrel moaned and sat forward in her chair. Charity went quickly to her side. "Are you alright?"

"I think so," Chyrel replied. "I must have dozed off."

"Maybe," Charity said, looking at her watch. "Both of us have been asleep for almost twenty minutes. We should go outside and check on the others." *Some kind of knock-out gas*, Charity thought, but not wanting to alarm the woman, she kept it to herself.

Outside, Charity looked toward the clearing. A light was on in the caretaker's house, and the director was still sitting at the table where she'd left him, though she was

certain that more than just a few minutes had passed. Chyrel stumbled from the door, and the two women walked toward the group.

"Fentanyl," Charity heard the director say. "That explains it."

Fentanyl? she thought, knowing she'd heard of it before.

"Ain't that the stuff the Russians used a coupla years ago?" Donnie Hinkle said. "The Dubrovka Theater?"

This confirmed the time discrepancy in Charity's mind. Donnie, an Australian by birth and former SEAL sniper, had been posted on a nearby island some time ago, and now he was suddenly here.

"Yeah," Director Stockwell replied as Kim McDermitt and Deputy Phillips approached the table. "A hundred and thirty hostages and all forty terrorists were killed by it." He nodded toward a metal can, similar to a propane tank. "Where'd you find this?"

Donnie jerked his thumb over his shoulder. "Floating on the bank next to the foot of the pier, Colonel."

Stockwell stood up and wobbled a little, as the rest of the team gathered around them. Charity noticed a cut on the back of his head, blood clotted in his closely cropped hair.

"A heavier-than-air gas," Stockwell said. "Must have been someone in scuba gear who released it on the north side, letting the breeze carry it over the whole island. Who was first to wake up?"

"The dog," Deputy Phillips replied. "Up on the deck."

"Makes sense," Andrew Bourke offered, his deep baritone voice seeming to echo across the island. Andrew, a handsome man with a barrel chest and thick mustache, had arrived on the chopper with Charity. "Had he been down here, he'd have been out longer. The rest of us were already asleep and didn't even notice it. How long were you knocked out?"

Two other men had arrived with Donnie and Andrew. Art Newman and Tony Jacobs were standing silently at the end of the table. They had just come on watch as Charity went to the cabin to look at the file. Both men were very capable former SEALs, as was their boss. Tony's shaved black head was beaded with perspiration.

Art looked at his wristwatch and said, "Tony and I just started our watch twenty-four minutes ago. I don't remember anything after my first circuit out to the north pier and back to where Donnie found me, and I woke up just a few minutes ago."

"So we were only out for fifteen or twenty minutes," Stockwell said. "They can't have gone far."

"The dive boat!" Kim shouted.

"What dive boat?"

"When Marty and I turned into Harbor Channel, there was a dive boat running without lights out beyond the Contents. The water's deeper out there, and it was headed east." She crossed her arms and looked around the group assembled around the table. On the verge of tears, she asked, "Where's my dad?"

Stockwell went over to where Kim stood, gently guiding her to the bench and sitting her down. "We'll find Jesse, Kim. You have my word on that."

Charity sat down and put her arm around the girl. "We will."

Stockwell started giving orders then. "Get Deuce on the horn," he told Chyrel and then turned to the young lawman. "Deputy, can you contact the sheriff? We need eyes in the sky. Did you see the dive boat as well?"

"Yes, sir, I'll give dispatch a description, and we'll have a chopper up out of Marathon right away. There may be others in Key Largo, and Key West also."

Stockwell reached into his pocket and took out a business card, handing it to Phillips. "Give the sheriff my number. Have him call me right away."

"Yes, sir," the deputy replied, taking the card and running across the clearing.

Stockwell slowly turned around toward Paul Bender, who'd been on the island when Charity and the others had arrived. Paul was a former Secret Service agent and had a degree in forensic psychology. "They came early, Paul. And covertly."

"They must have had a plan ahead of time. It's only twenty-one thirty. Lavolier and Horvac couldn't possibly have moved that fast. In fact, they should only have arrived in Marathon by now." He was talking about the leader of the Miami gang and the woman who somehow controlled him, that the group had rallied to protect Mc-Dermitt from.

"Andrew," Stockwell said, "get on the horn to the Coast Guard. Let them know one of our agents has been kidnapped." Formerly with the Coast Guard's vaunted Maritime Enforcement, Andrew now worked as the team's liaison with the Coast Guard.

"Linda!" Kim suddenly gasped. "Somebody has to call her."

"Do you have her number?" Tony asked calmly as he sat down next to Charity, nodding toward the chopper. "We'll call her together. Charity has to get up in the air."

As Charity rose and headed toward the chopper, Tony helped Kim to her feet and started toward Chyrel's office, which was now all lit up.

"Donnie, go with Andrew in the chopper," Stockwell ordered and turned to Bourke. "Andrew, coordinate with the Coast Guard and the sheriff's birds from the air. Have the sheriff's office pass the boat's description to every law enforcement agency between here and Miami."

Going over the preflight, while waiting for the others to gather their gear and get aboard, Charity thought long and hard about what she was about to do. Accepting the file from Director Stockwell had put things into motion that now couldn't be undone. At some point, she'd fly away from this group, and they'd be told she had stolen the helicopter and gone rogue.

Pushing thoughts about the future out of her mind, she concentrated on the immediate task at hand: finding Jesse McDermitt.

With the engine already running, Andrew and Donnie climbed aboard, Donnie in the back. He was still dressed all in black, after spending part of the night lying on a small stand on a nearby island with his sniper rifle and scope. From there, he could see nearly any approach to the island they were on—for all the good that had come of it. Apparently, the bad guys had gotten lucky and come from the opposite side of McDermitt's island from where Donnie had been perched. Everyone had thought the water to the north too shallow to warrant more than occasional observation from one of the two sentries.

Once airborne, Andrew got a text message from the director that their boss, Deuce Livingston, and several other team members had just touched down in Marathon in the company's Gulfstream and would split up there, two joining a sheriff's helo about to take off and two going back up in the G5, with its sophisticated radar, to act as command and control.

Livingston had been an officer in the Navy SEALs. He was Tony and Art's commanding officer, and both spoke very highly of him. He was an easygoing, good-natured man most of the time, but when times called for decisive leadership, that was when he was in his element. Tony had told Charity that the SEALs under his command would do anything he asked of them, relying on his intelligence and quick authoritativeness.

Within minutes, the men on the G-5 were back in the air and searching the area with radar, reporting quite a number of possible targets. Kumar Sayef, a twenty-year man and Delta Force linguist, was in command of the plane and began the arduous task of directing the two helicopters and eliminating the boats to the east of the island, one by one.

As the search progressed through the night, other helicopters and surface craft joined in. They'd intercepted and looked at more than ten boats already and were getting low on fuel.

Kumar had given them another boat to check out. "Roger that," Charity said. "We'll have to refuel after this one, if it's not the right boat." The only description they had for the target boat was that it was a white dive boat, about thirty feet in length, with a hard top that extended all the way to the stern. This had come from McDermitt's daughter and the deputy, who had seen a boat running without lights near the island just as they were returning to the island from their dinner date.

The next boat wasn't even close, a sailboat over forty feet in length. "Pulling off and heading to Marathon for fuel, Director," she informed Deuce's boss.

"Deuce is there getting fuel now," Stockwell said. "Agent Rosales should be arriving there any minute. Pick her up and bring her here before continuing the search."

She hauled back on the cyclic stick, and the helo went into a steep climb as she added throttle and pulled up on the collective. Climbing, she stepped on the right rotor pedal, moving the cyclic right and then forward, putting the bird into a tight, banking turn before diving back down toward the water.

Andrew had one hand on the handle by the door and the other on the dash in front of him, even though he was securely strapped in. "Where the hell did you learn to fly?" he asked through clenched teeth.

"Daddy was a helicopter pilot," Charity replied, offhandedly. "He flew in Vietnam and later as a crop duster. Some fields go right up to the tree line. I was flying before I got a license to drive a car."

Minutes later, they were on the ground in front of the fixed-base operator at Marathon airport. The fuel truck had just finished refueling the sheriff's bird that Deuce was in. When the fuel truck operator pulled up and began to refuel them, Charity climbed out with the two men, just as the sheriff's chopper was lifting off.

"I think my eyes are going crossed from looking at that little circle of light on the water for so long," Andrew said.

Looking toward the terminal building, Donnie pointed with his chin. "I reckon the tall Sheila headed this way's gonna be Jesse's lady friend."

Andrew broke apart and extended his hand. "I'm Andrew Bourke. You've met our pilot, Charity Styles, and this is Donnie Hinkle. We'll take you to the island before resuming the search."

Linda Rosales shook hands with all three. "I haven't talked to anyone since Kim called me two hours ago."

"Climb aboard, Linda," Charity said. "We're ready to go. Tony's with her and we'll fill you in on the way out there."

Linda climbed in back as Charity hurried around to the pilot's seat and started the engine. "Have you heard anything more?" Charity barely heard Linda ask. Donnie pointed to the headset he was wearing and another one hanging in front of the woman. Linda put it on and repeated the question.

"A lot of boats out there," Donnie replied. "But don't worry, love. We'll find him."

The big helicopter rose into the air quickly, the nose dipping as soon as they were aloft. Charity flew quickly along the short taxiway, gaining speed, then made a climbing turn over the runway before flying out over the water and turning northwest.

Charity gave Linda the details of the previous evening and the search they'd conducted so far. The flight to Jesse's island only took a few minutes.

McDermitt's mangrove-surrounded little island stood out against the other islands and black sea surrounding it, like a cruise ship floating on the water. The lights were on in all four structures, filling the center of the island with more than enough light, and torches were burning on the four corners, marking the inside edges of the dense vegetation around the perimeter of the island.

"We'll only be on the ground for a second, Linda," Charity said over the comm.

Andrew turned around in the copilot's seat as they descended. "We'll find him. You have my word."

Receiving the next location for yet another boat to look at from Kumar, Charity waited until Linda was out the door and clear, then quickly took off again and set a course for intercept. It was another false target, and she was beginning to think they'd never find the right one. She couldn't believe so many boats were out on the water in the middle of the night.

The director expanded the search area in all directions and announced that there were now six helos from the sheriff's department, Coast Guard, DEA, and FWC aiding in the search, plus twenty boats from all those agencies. Dozens of civilian boats were also hailing the Coast Guard, saying that they were heading out to join the search as well.

"Civilians?" Andrew asked nobody in particular.

"Jesse's pretty well thought of around these parts, mate," Donnie's voice came over the comm.

Charity remained silent, concentrating on flying and locating the next target. Her mind was also drifting to what lay ahead. DHS had already made a lot of arrangements and gone to considerable expense. When Stockwell had first approached her, she'd thought it over for a full two days before giving him her list of requirements. At the top of that list was to be able to use a sailboat to move around. And not just any sailboat. It would have to be big and heavy enough to take on occasional storms without putting into a port. And it also had to be small enough and rigged so that she could sail single-handed.

That meant a wooden sloop, forty feet or so. The design had to be simple, yet classic, to avoid drawing too much attention. It had to be completely set up with all the modern electronics equipment it could carry and have a number of hiding places built in to carry the things that a person could be arrested for in many countries.

Stockwell had simply nodded and taken notes. A week later, he'd contacted her again and told her that the DEA had acquired a forty-five-foot cutter-rigged sloop, designed by John Alden and built in a small shipyard in Wiscasset, Maine, in 1932. It had just finished being completely refitted in Miami.

The search for McDermitt continued, Charity locating and discounting seven more surface craft. The chopper's fuel tanks were nearly into reserves. Homestead was only a little further away than the airport in Marathon, as they were now searching the area north of Islamorada.

With less than an hour until daylight, Charity radioed that they were returning to Marathon to refuel. She wanted to be sure that when dawn broke, her tanks were full. The search could progress much faster once it was light, as the choppers could identify boat shapes and colors from a distance and not have to fly right up on them with spotlights.

Once they were on the ground, Andrew ran quickly to the general aviation building to get them some food while the tanker refueled the helo. She walked around to the other side of the chopper, where Donnie stood stretching.

"This don't look so good, love," he said as she came around the nose of the helicopter, drinking the last of the water from her bottle. "It's been eight hours now, and from the way it sounds, less than half the boats within range have been eliminated."

"It'll go faster once the sun comes up," Charity said.

"Jesse's a resourceful bloke. For all we know, the fellas that grabbed him are all dead now, their boat drifting aimlessly, and he's swimming back."

Charity only nodded. Looking around the airport, she was just able to make out the palm trees on the far side of the field now, as the first light of a new day approached.

Andrew came out of the terminal, carrying a box. "Water, energy drinks, and energy bars," he said, as he neared them. "Nothing here but vending machines."

Accepting a small energy drink, Charity drained most of it quickly, shaking her head and smacking her lips, from the sugary rush. Andrew put the box on the deck inside the back door of the bird and passed out energy bars and candy bars.

Charity finished a health food bar and crammed the wrapper in her pocket. "Let's get ready to get back up there. It'll be light enough to see the boats at a distance now."

The three of them strapped in, and Charity switched on the radio to contact Ralph Goodman, up in the G-5 with Kumar. Keying the mic, she said, "We're taking off in just a minute, Ralph. Where to next?"

"Charity, we found Jesse," the director's excited voice came back over her headset.

Motioning Andrew, she tapped her headset and said, "They found McDermitt!" As Donnie and Andrew put their headsets on, Charity ordered the fuel truck operator to stop and move away—they were taking off immediately.

The director continued, "He's near Marco Island and needs help. Get in the air as quickly as possible. Contact Tony and drop your passengers on his boat."

Once the fuel truck was clear, Charity started the engine and quickly spooled it up and raised the collective. She didn't bother with following the rules to fly over the taxiway and runway, but instead pointed the Huey due north, barely skimming the palm trees along the far side of the runway. Listening over the radio, she heard the director order two DEA choppers that were searching out beyond Key West to rendezvous and provide air support to the two boats that would arrive at the coordinates he gave.

Dropping the two men in the chopper onto a moving boat was something they'd trained to do many times, and it shouldn't present a problem on the calm sea below. Tony, Art, Paul, and Linda would be on McDermitt's Cigarette boat, heading straight toward the mainland.

Realizing that this would be the perfect opportunity for her to disappear gave Charity a sense of unease. She'd come to think of the people in their team as family. McDermitt was a good listener who had let her open up to him in her own time when the two had spent a couple of weeks alone on his big fishing boat, traveling all over the western Caribbean to find the man who had once been their boss.

Jason Smith had held a grudge against Livingston and McDermitt, blaming them for his being replaced and posted to the Horn of Africa. He'd hired mercenaries to kill them and nearly killed the president at the same time, and later he had been responsible for the bomb that had taken the life of Jared Williams, a Marine that McDermitt had been trying to help. Jared had suffered pretty severe post-traumatic stress over an incident that had been beyond his control in Iraq. He and Charity had bonded quickly when they'd first met.

When she and McDermitt had finally caught up to Smith, Charity had killed him with her bare hands, feeling no more remorse than if she'd squashed a roach.

Twenty miles north of Marathon, Charity spotted a big, fast-moving boat headed north-northeast on the radar and changed course to follow it.

In the back of the chopper, Donnie was breaking his rifle down and packing it in its case, preparing for the exchange. They'd made these kinds of transfers from chopper to boat many times, but never at the speed that they were preparing for now. Time was of the essence. The two men seemed confident in their ability, and Charity knew her flying skills were up to the task.

"I have the Cigarette on radar," Charity said over the intercom. "ETA is twenty minutes."

Bourke replied in his usual calm, deep voice. "If I don't get the chance to say it later, thanks for getting us on board safely."

Looking over at the big man in the copilot's seat, she only nodded. He was ten years older than she was, and Charity liked his easygoing manner and thought of him as the older brother she never had. He was always the cool head in any situation. During small boat boarding training, he'd been able to ease any anxiety she felt, the way he did now. Knowing that she might never see the man again gave her a feeling of regret and sadness.

Charity was glad that Tony would be at the helm of the boat, knowing he'd be talking constantly when they came over it, giving a running update on the sea ahead of him and how the boat would be handling.

Her job would be easy. Match their speed and let Art use hand signals to guide her to the right spot above their boat. Tony's running narrative would be more for Andrew and Donnie's benefit, but his calm way would help steady her at the controls.

Flying low, only a hundred feet off the water, she noted most of the images on her radar scope were headed south, so picking out the Cigarette boat heading north hadn't been difficult. There was one other boat heading north, about ten miles behind the Cigarette and on the same course, but moving about half the speed of the go-fast boat. A moment later, it came into view a few miles ahead.

"Is that—" Andrew began to say.

Charity finished his question. "Jesse's boat?" The Huey quickly closed on the much slower fishing boat, then flashed past it. "Sure is."

"That was his daughter at the helm!" Andrew exclaimed, reaching for the radio.

Charity touched his arm and stopped him. "What are you going to do? Order her to go back? Something tells me she's already been told that. Forget it, this thing will be over before she gets there, and she's not going to listen to reason." Andrew looked over at her. "You know I'm right, big guy," she added with a wink.

Andrew nodded, undid his harness, and climbed past her to the rear of the Huey. They'd be over the boat in just a few more minutes.

Charity turned on her earwig. All the team carried them and while they only had a five-mile range, they were near that now. "Tony, can you hear me?"

"Weak and broken," came his reply, punctuated by static.

"Five miles out," she said. "Rate of closure is forty-five knots."

"Roger, Charity," Tony replied, his voice coming through the tiny earpiece much clearer now. "Slowing to seventy knots. Damned sea is flat as glass. Never seen it so calm. We'll have to get Jesse to bring us all out here tomorrow and catch some fish."

Charity smiled, knowing that Tony was trying to ease the tension she and the men in back were feeling. That was just his way.

McDermitt had been taken against his will, but he must have escaped and somehow contacted Stockwell. She'd seen how quickly and violently McDermitt could react when someone crossed him. He wasn't the kind of man to make threats, intimidate, or mediate. Just swift and calculated action. If he was free, odds were good that whoever had taken him was hurting.

Pulling back on the cyclic while decreasing the collective, Charity brought the chopper's nose up slightly, slowing their airspeed as it descended. She looked back at Andrew and nodded.

The air inside the helo swirled suddenly, and a loud roar could be heard outside her headphones as Andrew opened the cargo door on the port side.

Being the heavier of the two, Andrew would go first. Charity slowed more and added just a little right pedal, while at the same time pushing the cyclic to the left. The two controls, used opposite, put the bird into angled flight, the nose pointing slightly to the right of their direction of travel.

Over the headphones, she heard Tony talking calmly to Andrew, but she was concentrating more on Art's hand signals. He was now standing in front of the passenger seat of the Cigarette, with Linda standing between them and Paul strapped into the port-side rear seat.

"Over the boat in ten seconds," she said over the intercom.

"Roger that, mate," Donnie replied. He and Andrew unplugged their comm link cables from the flight helmets they'd put on.

Though she couldn't see the men behind her, she knew that Andrew would be sitting on the edge of the deck, both feet planted firmly on the skids, and Donnie would be helping to steady him.

No longer even looking where she was going, Charity followed Art's signals and could feel the air change as her bird came down into the slipstream of the fast-moving boat. She made fine adjustments to the flight controls with a delicate hand, watching Art and feeling the way lower into the slipstream. Art continued to signal her forward with his left hand, his right hand held up at Andrew, palm out. Art then clenched his left fist, and

Charity held the controls steady, flying at seventy knots about five feet above the boat.

Though she couldn't see it, she felt the weight of the helo change as Andrew jumped. She instinctively corrected for the difference and heard a grunt over her earwig as he dropped to the deck below.

The helo, now lighter, had moved just a bit off station, and Charity corrected for it, following Art's patient signals. A moment later, he again clenched his left fist, and she felt the helo lighten once more. A second later, Art gave her a thumbs-up, and she peeled off, setting a course for Homestead.

CHAPTER FOUR:

A wad Qureshi woke with a start. Through the tent's screen window, he could see that it was still dark outside. A noise had disturbed his sleep, but now he heard nothing. Their camp was dark, as fires were only permitted inside the rim of the old volcano's peak.

Awad listened intently for a moment but heard nothing but silence. Then came the low, rolling rumble of distant thunder, far off in the distance.

Pushing a button on his wristwatch, he looked at the illuminated dial and saw that it was still an hour before the sun would be up. Wide awake, he realized it would be pointless to try to go back to sleep. Instead, he sat up, put on his boots and rose from the cot.

Outside, he saw Karim Majdi sitting alone on a log in front of the half circle of tents. Most of the tents were larger and housed two men. Only he, Majdi, and Hussein had separate tents to themselves.

Reaching back inside, Awad picked up the small pack, identical to the ones they all carried, and started toward Karim. Clearing his throat to keep from alarming him, Awad approached and then sat down on the log beside the older man. Karim was twenty-eight and had been living in the town of Waco, Texas, for seven years, working as a mechanic. Short and slight of build, with hair just touching his shoulders in the typical American fashion, he was the son of a tribal elder.

"*As-salamu alaykum*, Karim," Awad greeted the man.

Karim only nodded, taking a drag from a cigarette. Exhaling into the night sky, he said, "The storm woke you?"

"Yes, do you think it will rain today?" Though Waco was nearly fifteen hundred kilometers to the north, Karim had told him once that the arid mountainous area they were hiding in was similar to that surrounding the Texas city.

"I don't believe so," Karim whispered. "It is far to the east. Out over the ocean, I think. Did Hussein give you the details last night?"

Though they were supposed to be working together, Awad knew that Hussein wouldn't divulge everything to everyone and thought that Karim might be trying to trick him into saying something he shouldn't.

"Have you been to San Antonio?" Awad asked quietly, as if making conversation.

Karim nodded. "Many times. I have even been there for their military festival and have ridden on the boats that will be our target."

"What is it like? Will there be many people there?"

"Hundreds," Karim replied. "Perhaps thousands. Hussein has chosen a good target. The infidels will be there with their families, reveling in their debauchery. It is unlikely that anyone in the crowd will be armed. It will be glorious."

Awad considered this. He'd hoped the mission would be against the military or law enforcement. He'd only been in America a short time, but could already see how he could easily adopt the Western lifestyle. Karim had lived among them for seven years, yet still held fast to his ideology.

"Yes," Awad finally agreed. "A glorious triumph for Allah."

"*Allahu Akbar*," Karim said quietly, but with great conviction.

Changing the subject, Awad asked, "What are the plans for today?"

"More shooting practice," Karim replied. "The weapons we are using are not very accurate, but they have great capacity and are small enough to easily conceal. We must become more proficient with their use to be effective."

Just then, a movement caused them both to turn. Stepping out of one of the tents, the man who had been doing the cooking for the group started toward them. He only nodded as he passed and headed up the trail to the crater, carrying his pack over his shoulder. If all was clear, he'd light the cook fire to prepare breakfast for the men.

"I think I will go and help," Awad said as he stood up.

Karim grinned. "You are going only to be first in line for the food."

Shrugging, Awad nodded and started up the path, following the cook. The truth was, since Hussein's revelation of the civilian target, he just wasn't sure about anything any more.

When he reached the area in the crater where they usually ate, he found the cook there, the fire already going. The spot was surrounded by large boulders, open only on one side, so it was nearly invisible from further down inside the massive basin.

Fareed Basara saw Awad approaching as he cut up a large piece of meat for the morning stew. He only nodded at the younger man.

"I thought I might be of assistance," Awad said.

Fareed only grunted an acknowledgment as he carefully cut the meat in the near darkness. Fareed was the oldest of the group, two years older than Hussein. He came from a nomadic tribe in the Pamir Mountain range, near Afghanistan's border with Pakistan and China. Being a nomad, he'd learned from childhood how to cook and prepare food.

Fareed stopped what he was doing and looked up at the younger man. "What is America like?"

Awad considered the question a moment. "There are as many different parts to it as there are rocks on Shah Foladi," he replied, referring to the highest peak in the Hindu Kush range. "Yet with all their differences, they are still all the same."

"Do you like it?"

Again, Awad felt as if he were being tested. "Most of them are a decadent people. Trapped by an overabundance of technology. They have forgotten how to do the simple things, such as you are doing now. They eat in restaurants, both fine and sickening, allowing strangers to prepare and handle their food."

Placing a kettle on a hook over the fire, Fareed said, "Will you bring that water container and pour a liter into the pot for me?"

Awad did as he was bid, bringing one of the many twenty-liter water cans from its hiding place among the rocks. As he poured a small amount into the cauldron, it began to boil furiously, then slowed and finally stopped.

Fareed waited a moment, allowing the water to begin bubbling once more, before sliding the meat from a makeshift cutting board into the kettle. From another hiding place, Fareed retrieved a small, sealed container and dumped the whole contents in with the meat. It contained a number of vegetables that Fareed had either bought or collected along the way, along with a few spices he'd purchased in a small Muslim store in Mexico City when he'd first arrived.

The two men sat down in silence, Fareed occasionally stirring the stew with a long wooden spoon, which he'd carved from a green sapling. After thirty minutes, he lifted the kettle off the fire and placed it on a flat rock, heated by the fire. He did this so the stew could cool enough to be eaten, but not get completely cold.

Soon, the others began to arrive, each carrying his own bowl in his small canvas pack. Also in the packs were the Russian-made Bizon SMG machine pistols each of them had been given.

CHAPTER FIVE:

Burrs Strip was an ideal location to keep the Huey, Charity realized upon landing. Located in the outskirts of South Miami Heights, it had a grass airstrip and a small hangar, where engine work was done. The whole field was surrounded by mature avocado trees. DHS had leased a section of the hangar to store the chopper on a long-term basis. Charity left the bird on the ground outside the hangar, knowing that it would be wheeled inside as soon as someone arrived in about an hour.

From the airstrip, it was only a quarter-mile walk through a quiet residential neighborhood to the safe house, also leased on a long-term basis. Taking only her go-bag, Charity reached the house in minutes. It was a typical South Florida home, stucco walls and red barrel-tile roof, with reflective tinting on the windows to keep out the hot sub-tropical sun.

Looking up and down the street and not seeing anyone, she hurried to the door and unlocked it. The sun wasn't completely up yet, but it was already getting light outside. She hadn't seen any of the neighbors as she'd walked here, and had heard only one dog bark.

Quickly checking each room of the house, she then went straight to the kitchen. The refrigerator and pantry held little, just bottled water and nonperishable canned food.

It doesn't matter, she thought. Her plan was to take a quick shower, eat a snack, take a short nap and arrive at the marina at noon.

Opening the door from the kitchen to the garage, she found a nondescript silver Hyundai minivan parked there, the keys to which were hanging on a hook just inside the kitchen door. Sometime later in the day, or early tomorrow, an agent from the CIA would pick up the van and return it to the safe house. They were used to these kinds of things, and Director Stockwell had arranged and planned everything for her disappearance.

Digging through the canned foods in the pantry, she found a fruit cocktail and ate it quickly, straight from the can. The boat, she knew, would be well provisioned, and she'd only need to stop at a grocery store to get some frozen meats, vegetables, and fresh fruit before departing Florida, maybe for the last time.

Going to the large walk-in closet in the master bedroom, Charity found two matching suitcases in a corner, both empty. Against the far wall was a dresser, and on the right, a shoe rack with two pairs of boat shoes and a pair of jungle boots, matching the ones she was wearing. Opening the top drawer of the dresser, she found an assortment of T-shirts and tank tops, all her size. In the second drawer, she found socks, panties, and bras of assorted colors, all name brands and, again, all the right size. Obviously, the director had had a woman do the clothes shopping, judging from the second drawer's contents. In the third and fourth drawers, she found several pairs of shorts, long-sleeved work shirts like McDermitt always wore, and several pairs of women's long pants.

It only took her a few minutes to pack, leaving out a pair of khaki shorts, a blue tank top, a bra and panties, placing them on a recliner in the bedroom. Before closing the last case, she placed the target's file folder on top. Carrying both suitcases to the garage, she put them in the back of the minivan.

Back in the bedroom, she went straight to the bathroom, stripping off her clothes as she went. Below the sink she found a small overnight case, and in the medicine cabinet were a new toothbrush, toothpaste, scent-free deodorant, one pair of latex gloves, and a single bottle of jet-black hair dye.

Standing in just her bra and panties, Charity looked at herself in the mirror. Since Afghanistan, she'd worn her hair cropped very short, no longer desiring the attention. She'd let it grow these last few months, and it was now past her shoulders. Her naturally blond tresses were something she'd been proud of when she was younger. Now, her hair color would be a detriment to the mission.

Reading the directions on the back of the bottle, she put on the gloves and quickly worked the dye into her hair and scalp for several minutes, a towel around her shoulders.

For the next twenty minutes, while she waited for the dye to set, she padded barefoot through the house, inspecting each room more closely and going through the dressers and closets. All the rooms were tastefully furnished, but none of the drawers or closets contained anything at all.

As she passed back through the living room, she looked out the big picture window and saw an old man on the sidewalk. He just stood there, looking at the house. At first, she thought he was some kind of pervert, but then remembered the windows were tinted and she'd been unable to see inside when she'd approached the house.

The man started to walk up the driveway, then seemed to decide against it and turned around. He was nearly back to the sidewalk and stopped again, seeming to look through the tinted window at her.

"Keep going, old man," Charity mumbled under her breath.

After a moment, the silver-haired man started back up the driveway again.

"Shit!" She'd need to think fast. He'd obviously seen her arrive. Maybe he was a nosy neighbor, or just someone who looked out for everyone in the neighborhood.

The doorbell rang. Charity couldn't ignore it. He might call the police. She decided to improvise and strode purposefully to the door, tossing the towel on the floor and removing her bra.

One of the team members, a former CIA spook and master of disguise, had trained the rest of them on the best ways not to be seen and—if that failed—how not to be remembered. He said that the best way to not be recognized was to draw attention away from the face. That shouldn't be too hard, dressed only in black panties.

As Charity quickly pulled open the door, she said, "You're early, stud."

The old man gasped, his eyes going straight to Charity's bare breasts and taut, flat belly. She quickly closed the door partway and hid behind it.

"Oh God! I'm so sorry, sir. I thought you were my husband."

The man turned partly away, holding a hand to the side of his face in embarrassment. "Dear me! I'm very sorry. I saw you go in a bit ago and the house had been empty for quite a while, I was suspicious. I'm terribly sorry!"

"We just b-bought it," Charity said, pretending to be flustered, still hiding behind the door. "My husband's a pilot and I'm a flight attendant, Mister...?"

"Jimenez," the old man said, still shielding his eyes. "Walter Jimenez. I'm the block captain."

"I'm terribly sorry, Mister Jimenez. I thought I'd be surprising my husband."

"It is I who should be sorry, ma'am."

"Gabriela," Charity said. "My friends call me Gabby. Gabby Fleming. If you'll give me a second to grab a robe, you may come in."

"No, no, that's quite alright, Missus Fleming. Perhaps another time. When your husband is home."

"If he's ever home, you mean. Like I said, we both work for American Airlines and see each other more in hotels than anywhere else. In fact, we'll be allowing coworkers to stay here from time to time."

"Again, I'm terribly sorry, Missus Fleming. I really must be going now."

"Very nice to meet you, Mister Jimenez," Charity said as she closed the door and smiled. Satisfied that the man never saw her face, she locked the door and went quickly to the bathroom, gathering her bra and the wet towel as she went.

Showering and rinsing her hair thoroughly, Charity towel-dried her now jet-black hair. Taking a clean towel from the bathroom closet, she pulled down the new-looking comforter on the bed.

The sheets were obviously brand-new, the creases still visible. As tired as she was, the bed appeared cool and inviting. She folded the towel double and placed it on the pillow, then set the alarm on the nightstand for noon. Finally, she lay down on the big bed, completely nude. She'd been awake, except for the short gas-induced nap, for more than twenty four hours. With the quiet hum of the air conditioner and steady beat of the ceiling fan, she made a mental note to tell the director about the visitor and her cover story, then was soon fast asleep.

CHAPTER SIX:

It seemed like only a few minutes later when Charity snapped instantly awake, drenched in a cold sweat. It took a moment for her to recall her surroundings. She was in a big, comfortable king-sized bed in a safe house in Miami, not tied across a table, being sodomized by one of the filthy Taliban fighters who'd captured her in Afghanistan.

The dreams came less frequently now than they used to, but after having one, she'd always smell the stench of the guards' body odors. The cave they'd kept her in had smelled of rotten garbage, excrement, and urine.

At first, she'd been stretched across a rough wooden table, flat on her belly with her hands and feet tied to the table legs. She'd been kept like that throughout the first night, so some of the smell was her own body odor and waste. During that first night she'd been repeatedly raped, beaten, and sodomized, at least half a dozen times, by several different men.

Jared had once told her his secret to combating the terrible dreams he'd once had. He'd told her to never let her guard down, always keep pushing at whatever it was you were doing to wear your mind and body out.

Though he was four years younger than Charity, she'd fallen for his rugged, yet innocent independence. Like McDermitt, he was a Marine sniper and a very good one. A powerfully built man, he'd also been incredibly gentle. Their first night together, they'd just drifted on one of McDermitt's boats, heads propped on life vests, while they lay on their backs, staring up at the night sky.

Jared could name many of the individual stars and planets, and could point out the various constellations, telling the story behind each. She'd told him that she'd simply never been able to discern the shapes early man had seen in the night sky. He'd then told her to close her eyes, and he described how the image looked in every detail. Then he'd told her to open her eyes and pointed to a cluster of stars. She'd seen the picture he'd painted in her mind, with his soft country-boy accent, in every detail then.

In the hours before dawn, they'd made love while drifting beneath that blanket of stars. She'd been the one to initiate it, and he'd been her first, since Afghanistan. In her mind, she could still see his face and hear his voice.

Two days after that night, Jared had been killed in an explosion meant to kill them all, sacrificing his own life, pushing at what it was he did best. Protecting others.

Several days after Jared's funeral, in the middle of the night, Charity had left with McDermitt on his boat. It had taken them nearly two weeks, crisscrossing the Caribbean, but they'd finally found the man responsible, and she'd killed him herself. Paralyzed him first with a powerful roundhouse kick to the base of the skull and then, with her bare hands, as he lay helpless on the ground, she'd snapped his neck, like a dry twig.

During the return to Florida, Charity had had the dream again and woken, screaming in the guest cabin. McDermitt had found her sobbing, knees curled up to her chest. The two of them had sat on the bridge of the big boat the rest of that night, drinking his strong coffee, as the boat sliced through the water toward home. She'd told him about her feelings for Jared and how she'd thought killing the man responsible for his death would give her closure, but it hadn't.

McDermitt had told her a little about his own background, but mostly he'd just listened. The man was a very good listener. The kind of person who could elicit more information from you with no more than an arch of his eyebrow.

Rising from the bed, Charity had a sudden pang of guilt for leaving the way she had. She still didn't know if McDermitt and the other members of her team were safe. She knew he was still alive. He'd struck her as an extremely resilient man, one that would take an awful lot of effort to kill.

She turned off the alarm, noting that it would be going off in just minutes. She went straight to the shower, turned on the cold water and stepped quickly under it. Gasping, she placed her hands on the wall, leaning toward it and letting the cold water cascade over the back of her head and down her body, washing away the filth she imagined there.

Stepping out minutes later, she dried quickly, went to the recliner in the corner of the bedroom and got dressed. It took her ten minutes to go through the whole house, wiping everything she'd touched with the wet towel. In the kitchen, she washed out the empty can she'd eaten from and put it in her purse, to discard later. She wiped the faucet handles, took the keys from the hook and opened the door with the towel.

A minute later, Charity put on her dark wraparound sunglasses and backed the minivan out of the garage, clicking the remote for the garage door mounted on the visor when the car was clear. Driving south for ten blocks, she didn't see many people. It was a working-class neighborhood, and the only sign of life was a two-man yard crew at work near the end of the street. They didn't seem to notice the nondescript minivan as it rolled slowly down the street.

Turning left onto Old Cutler Road, Charity kept the car at the speed limit for almost a mile before turning right onto 112th Avenue. A few blocks later, she turned into a Publix supermarket to get the perishable provisions she'd need for the next week. She was relieved to see the grocery store parking lot wasn't crowded. She deposited the empty can and the towels she'd used to dry off and wipe down the house into a trash can before going into the store.

She moved quickly to the produce section, loading fruits and vegetables in her cart. They wouldn't keep long, but she planned to eat fresh food for the first few days of her journey and only resort to the canned stuff she knew to be on the boat as a last resort. In the meat market, she picked out several packages of frozen chicken breasts and pork chops. Moving to the hair care section, she picked out both black and blond hair dye, along with black root touchup. Minutes later, she loaded the groceries into the back of the car and drove off.

When Charity arrived at Black Point Marina, she chose a parking spot away from the marina office, shaded from the afternoon sun by a royal poinciana tree. The marina was large, the biggest in Miami, in fact. It being a weekday, the parking lot, with its long drive-through spaces for trucks pulling boat trailers, was nearly empty.

Her home and transportation was in a slip near the end of the furthest pier, with no other slips occupied for half the length of the dock. Carrying the groceries, she stepped down into the boat's cockpit, enjoying for a moment the familiar solid feel and elegant lines of the old sailboat. Her uncle on her father's side had a boat just like this.

Well, she thought, *not exactly like this one.*

Placing the bags on the deck near the hatch, Charity knelt and opened a small recessed panel in the low bulkhead of the cabin roof. Punching in the four-digit code, she watched the light change from red to green and heard a solid thunk as the deadbolts on either side of the roof hatch released.

The hatch cover slid back easily, and to her surprise, the lower panel, part of the aft bulkhead, slid down into a recess. Charity looked around and, seeing no one, she picked up the grocery bags and stepped quickly down the ladder into the salon. The temperature below deck was quite a bit cooler, being that most of the heavy boat was beneath the water line.

The interior layout was much like her uncle's Alden. A small navigation desk to starboard and a tiny galley to port, with an L-shaped countertop which extended amidships, and below which was the propulsion engine. To the rear of the galley and nav station, two small quarter berths extended, each beneath the bench seats of the cockpit.

The quarter berth aft the galley had a thick door installed, as it had been converted to a small generator compartment and dry goods storage. The gen-set powered the electrical system, including air conditioning, and kept the batteries charged while under sail. Accessing it would mean pulling everything off the shelves and folding them up out of the way, as it was located below the cockpit deck.

Aft the nav station, the smaller quarter berth had been converted into a built-in refrigerator and freezer forward, with room enough for two weeks of frozen food. The aft part of the berth had been converted to a storage locker, accessed by raising the top of the starboard bench seat in the cockpit. Being familiar with the layout, she could picture the many hiding places throughout the boat which the director had told her about.

She booted up the laptop on the desk of the nav station and inserted the thumb drive that was on the car's key ring. It held more detailed files, which she'd download to the computer so she could later study all the refit items the boat had undergone.

Forward of the galley and nav station was the salon, which looked nearly identical to her uncle's. Matching couches faced one another, port and starboard. Beneath these she knew there would be fuel, water, and holding tanks. Attached to the massive wooden mast, which extended up through the cabin roof and down through the sole to the keel, a narrow table separated the couches with folding sides. When raised, the table reached from one couch to the other.

On the port side of the mast, the bulkhead held a flat-screen TV, and below that were cabinets for storing DVDs and CDs. Behind the racks of recorded entertainment, she knew there was a long hidden compartment. It extended the width of the head on the other side of the bulkhead, with the marine toilet raised slightly above it. There she knew she'd find the gun case, holding the very Barrett sniper rifle she'd been training with for three months.

Charity quickly put the meat into the freezer drawer aft the nav station. The boat was connected to shore power to maintain the batteries, and the freezer was humming quietly and already very cold. The vegetables went into the tiny crisper in the refrigerator drawer just above it. The fruit she stored in several hanging nets around the galley, easy to get to for a quick snack.

Back at the nav station, she inserted the ignition key and started the brand-new Yanmar diesel engine to allow it time to warm up. The engine ran so quiet, it was barely heard above the hum of the reefer. Glancing at the gauges, she satisfied herself that everything was functioning as it should and climbed back up the ladder to retrieve her luggage.

"Ahoy," came a man's voice from the dock, startling her. Instinctively, her right hand went behind her, for the pistol tucked in her shorts at the small of her back.

Regaining her composure, she looked up at a man who looked to be in his early twenties. He was tall, dark-tanned, and fit, wearing white shorts, a blue golf shirt with the marina logo on the left breast and dark sunglasses.

"Hello," Charity said with a slight, but fake, Cuban accent.

"I saw you arrive. Are you heading out?"

For a moment, she wondered if the director had missed something, forgotten to pay some fee, perhaps.

"Yes," she replied cheerfully, studying the younger man from behind her dark sunglasses. "I am meeting friends on Key Biscayne, and we're cruising the Bahamas for a few weeks."

"Sounds like a great way to usher in the summer," he said. "Will you need anything from the marina?"

Charity relaxed a little and smiled. "No, I don't believe so."

"A hand casting off?"

She thought about it a moment. He'd seen her arrive, probably knew her car and, even with the shades on, knew what she looked like. There was nothing she could do now but go along.

"If you could give me a hand with my luggage first, I would very much appreciate it."

"*Un placer, señorita.*"

Charity turned up the smile and the charm, figuring that's what was expected. "*Hablas español?*" she asked as she climbed up onto the deck of the cockpit.

The young man smiled broadly, and Charity knew that behind his sunglasses, he was looking her up and down. "Not a lot, but everyone in South Florida speaks a little."

Pointing behind the man, she said, "I am parked there."

As they walked toward the minivan, the man said, "I'm Kevin. I don't remember seeing you around."

"I am Gabriela," Charity said, using her alias. "My father had the boat brought here. I only flew in last night."

She opened the hatchback and started to stretch for one of the larger bags, but Kevin reached in and took both of the larger ones. "Allow me. It's quite a beautiful boat."

Picking up the overnight bag, Charity closed and locked the car. "Yes, it is, thank you. It is a John Alden design, built in 1932. You are familiar with Alden?"

"I've heard of him," Kevin replied, "and seen pictures of boats he designed, but yours is the first I've seen up close."

Walking toward the dock, Charity decided the man wasn't a threat to either her or her mission. "He was probably the best naval architect America ever produced," she said, reciting her uncle's familiarity with the man. "His designs are clean and simple on the outside, yet very elegant. Most Alden-designed boats were built to be single-handed. I learned to sail her when I was only a child."

When Charity stepped aboard, Kevin stopped and started to place the luggage on the pier.

"Would you hand them down to me please?" she asked and, without waiting for an answer, stepped quickly through the hatch and down the ladder.

In the salon, she put the overnight bag on the counter and picked up her purse, taking out a crisp twenty-dollar bill and putting it in her pocket. She returned to the hatch, where the young man squatted, peering inside.

Removing his sunglasses, he said, "Wow! This is absolutely beautiful."

"Thank you," she said, noticing his bright blue eyes as he handed her the first suitcase.

Already very familiar with her cover story, she told it just as she'd rehearsed. "My family made our escape from Cuba in this very boat during the confusion of the Mariel boatlift. Father recently had her completely refitted before he gave her to me. Tomorrow will be her first day in the open ocean since he sailed her from Cuba when I was a small child."

"That was before I was born," Kevin said, handing down the second bag. "Why did he never sail her again?"

"Oh, we sailed a lot," she replied. "We just never sailed in the ocean. Father was always afraid the Cuban government would catch him."

"You were probably too young to remember anything about Cuba," he said. Charity knew he was trying to be flattering and making an advance.

She smiled as she started up the ladder. "Yes, I was only four years old," she lied, adding a few years. "But I remember some things."

Kevin stood and stepped back as Charity emerged from the cabin. "I'll disconnect the shore power, if you'll untie the lines and hold her fast for a moment."

A moment later, the boat was free of its tethers, Kevin holding the rail as she stepped back aboard. "It was a pleasure to meet you, Kevin," Charity said, extending her hand with the bill tucked in it.

He took her hand and casually palmed the bill, putting it into his own pocket. "*El placer ha sido todo mío, Señorita Gabriela.*"

Charity smiled as she slid onto the narrow bench behind the helm and opened the control panel in the wheel pedestal. The wheel itself was mounted forward the pedestal, and there were hooks on either side to tether the pilot in foul weather. Inside the pedestal was an array of gauges and switches, with a large compass mounted on top of it.

She nodded to the young man, who released his hold on the rail and gave the heavy boat a gentle nudge away from the pier. Charity engaged the transmission for a few seconds to start the boat moving out of the slip. Flipping a switch on the console, she waited a moment while the watertight covers on the bow thruster opened, then toggled the control to shove the bow around. Closing the thruster doors, she then reengaged the transmission, idling slowly around the end of the piers toward the canal that led into Biscayne Bay.

Clearing the point where the marina office was located, she glanced over. Kevin was standing on the fuel dock and waving. She smiled and waved back before throttling up slightly, anxious to get to the deeper water of the bay. At just four knots, it took nearly half an hour to reach the outer markers at the channel entrance.

Though the old wooden boat could be single-handed fairly well back when it was new, it was much easier to do so now, with the aid of the new electronics and automatic systems that had been installed. Once clear of the last marker, she used the automatic controls to raise the mainsail and unfurl the staysail. Although the mast was original and as big as a tree trunk, reaching sixty feet up toward the sky, the boom was aluminum, with a fully automated boom furler.

With the main and forestay close hauled and in irons, both sails luffing in the light wind, she turned slightly off the easterly breeze to the north and shut off the engine. The sails snapped as the light air filled them. The weight of the wind on the sails heeled the boat over, and Charity felt a rush of adrenaline, the same feeling of elation she'd felt as a young woman, sailing with her father and uncle, whenever their boat's sails had filled.

The heavy boat slowed momentarily in the turn, losing the momentum the engine provided, then gaining it back as the sails filled. The winches for the running rigging could be controlled automatically by the computer, constantly adjusting sail position for changing wind conditions to maintain the most efficient attitude. But Charity preferred to sail by feel and hadn't engaged the automated system. The winches were completely under her control, and she adjusted the main, moving the boom outboard until the mainsail began to luff slightly, then hauling it back in a few inches.

Her destination for now lay just across Biscayne Bay, seven miles due east, but with the easterly wind, she'd tack northeast to the halfway point, then jibe back to the southeast. The crossing would only take a couple of hours, then she'd anchor in the lee of Boca Chita Key. There she intended to spend the rest of the day familiarizing herself with the boat and its two million dollars' worth of upgrades while waiting for the early-morning high tide. Then she'd retire to the forward berth for a good night's sleep.

In the morning, two hours before daylight, the tide would peak and the outgoing current through Lewis Cut would help carry the boat into the Atlantic Ocean, under cover of darkness.

Halfway across the bay, Charity made the tack southeast, the boat responding beautifully. She took her satellite phone out of her pocket, pulled up the director's secure number and punched the call button.

"Are you aboard?" Stockwell whispered as the connection was made.

"Just departed the marina," she replied. "How's the search going?"

"McDermitt signaled us using a laser bore sighter, if you can believe it."

"He's safe, then?" she asked, relieved.

"Yes, everything was wrapped up within a couple of hours of your disappearance. A few bad guys were killed, but none of the team was hurt. Agent Rosales killed Tena Horvac."

The tension she'd felt about leaving the group in the way she had was suddenly lifted. "Thanks, Director."

"And that will be the last time you call me that," Director Stockwell said. "From now on, you call me Uncle. Now go. Sail away and do what you've been training for."

CHAPTER SEVEN:

It was midafternoon when Charity dropped anchor at Boca Chita Key, a tiny island about ten miles south of Key Biscayne. Though uninhabited, it was part of the Biscayne National Park and used as a rustic campground by boaters. The island had a small harbor, but Charity chose to anchor on the west side until she could be sure the water was deep enough to enter.

The entrance to the harbor was only seven feet deep at high tide. *Dancer's* draft was six feet, much too close to take the risk except at the peak of high tide. Even with the sophisticated forward- and side-scanning sonar system on board, she didn't want to chance it.

The large Danforth anchor bit into the sandy bottom as she backed down hard on it. With the wind blowing from the island and the tide rising, there was little chance of the boat swinging around.

Searching several yachting sites online, she soon learned that the tide here peaked an hour and twenty-four minutes after the high tide shown for Government Cut in Miami. Checking the tide chart for the Cut, she calculated that it was still an hour from the tidal peak. The next high tide, then, would be twelve hours and thirty minutes later, just before sunrise.

Standing on the cabin roof in front of the mast, Charity looked over the island through her binoculars. There was one boat tied up to the concrete dock that encircled the harbor, a pilothouse trawler about forty feet long. Being a deep-draft boat, it probably wouldn't be leaving before high tide, if at all.

She decided to hail the boat, knowing they had to be aware she was anchored just outside the harbor. Pulling her handheld marine band VHF radio from the clip on her belt, she keyed the mic. "This is *Wind Dancer* calling the pilothouse trawler in Boca Chita Harbor."

She waited a moment and then a woman's voice answered back, "This is *Sea Biscuit*. Are you the sloop anchored just outside?"

"Yes, I'm waiting for high tide before entering. Will you be leaving on the tide?"

"No, *Wind Dancer*. We're here for a couple of days. Feel free to come in whenever you want. The channel's deeper than the charts say. It was eight feet on the morning tide."

"Thanks, *Sea Biscuit*."

Charity waited a moment longer, looking at the boat through the binoculars. Finally, a woman and a young girl about nine or ten stepped out onto the dock. The woman was tall and athletic. She turned and waved before following the girl down a trail and disappearing into the brush.

A moment later, Charity sat at the nav station, familiarizing herself with the many upgrades in the boat's automated systems. After an hour of reading over the files, she started the engine, certain she could sail the boat anywhere she wanted to go.

Back at the helm, Charity nudged the boat forward as the windlass pulled the anchor free of the sandy bottom. Switching the sonar to forward scan, she saw the bottom and sides of the channel displayed in full color on the small screen, showing more than a foot of clearance to the bottom, with no irregularities.

Navigating the channel proved to be very easy, using the bow thruster for minor corrections. Not wanting to be intrusive, she chose a spot thirty or forty feet behind the trawler and brought the boat to a stop, the fenders still a foot from the black rubber bumpers on the concrete seawall.

Leaping the short span with both the stern and bow lines in hand, she pulled on both until the fenders lightly bumped the dock. The woman had reappeared, sitting alone on the fly bridge of the trawler. Charity finished tying the lines off, fore and aft, then stood and looked around.

"You made that channel look easy," the woman shouted from the sundeck of the trawler.

"Thanks," Charity called back. Remembering how cordial the cruising people she'd met in her youth had been she started walking toward the other boat. "The bow thruster helps. I'm Gabriela."

The woman quickly descended the ladder and vaulted the low wooden rail that ran the length of the boat. Striding toward her in bare feet, she extended her hand. "Savannah. Savannah Richmond."

Charity took the woman's hand and said, "Gabriela Fleming. My friends call me Gabby."

"Then that's what I'll call you, Gabby. Are you sailing alone?"

"Yes, for now. I'm meeting friends in Key Biscayne in the morning, but I don't like crowds."

"Same with us," Savannah said. "It's just me and my daughter, Flo. She's over on the beach, looking for clams."

Savannah was older than Charity first thought, by probably a decade. Tall and slim, with broad shoulders and a deep tan, she had naturally blond hair streaked by years of sun and water. Dressed in a pair of well-worn jeans and a lightweight white long-sleeved top, she was taller than Charity by a few inches, even in bare feet.

"Care to come aboard and get out of the sun?" Savannah asked. "I just put some beer in the cooler up on the fly bridge."

Not wanting to seem uncordial, Charity accepted, and the two women stepped over the gunwale and climbed a short ladder to the covered sundeck. Besides the captain's chair, there was ample seating and reclining room for several people.

Savannah handed Charity a cold beer from the cooler, then sat down on the full recliner aft the captain's chair, stretching her legs out and nodding toward the recliner opposite. "Have a seat, Gabby. I like to sit up here, where I can see better. Last night's sunset was spoiled by a storm out over the Glades. Tonight should be better."

Charity sat down and relaxed a little. "Where are you from?" she asked casually.

"I'm originally from Beaufort, South Carolina. But since Flo's first birthday, this boat and wherever we anchored has been our home."

"Is Flo short for something?" Charity asked, already guessing what it was.

"Family tradition," Savannah replied with a grin. "Mom and Dad are Madison and Jackson, my sister's name is Charlotte and now we have Florence."

Looking out to port, Charity could see the beach on the far side of the island and the little girl wading in the shallow water collecting clams. She surmised that the fly bridge was Savannah's favorite spot so she could keep an eye on her daughter, more than to watch the sunset.

"Your boat is beautiful, Gabby," Savannah said after taking a long pull on the cold beer bottle. "Looks like an Alden design."

"It is," Charity replied, keeping to her slight Cuban accent. "She was built in 1932, but recently refitted. I love this old trawler of yours."

"Thank you. It's a Grand Banks forty-two-foot Classic. Also, refitted recently. My husband and I split up several times, but for some strange reason, I always went back to him. The last time was just after Flo was born. While he was out sowing his oats again, I packed up and went home to my folks. Dad gave me *Sea Biscuit* and said if I stayed away from the asshole for a year, his words, he'd do a complete refit. I did, and when the divorce was final, Flo and I moved aboard and hoisted anchor. I don't think I could ever go back now. What about you? Ever married?"

"No," Charity replied. "A couple of boyfriends, nothing serious. I thought one might be the right guy, but he died several months ago." She regretted saying it as soon as the words left her mouth.

Savannah sat up and looked deeply into the younger woman's eyes. "I'm so sorry, Gabby."

"It is alright. Perhaps one day, maybe." Then, changing the subject, Charity asked, "Where are you heading?"

"We just returned from the Bahamas," Savannah replied. "We'd been cruising there for two years. Now we're heading to the Keys. Maybe look up an old friend or two."

The faraway look in Savannah's eyes told Charity that the *old friend* was a long-lost lover. "When were you last there?" Charity asked, sipping her beer.

"It's been a long time," Savannah replied. "Late 1999, but still hurricane season. My sister and I were on our way to Key West in our dad's boat. We'd hired a captain, so we could just enjoy the cruise. Char ended up skipping out on me, so I decided to send the captain home and stayed over in Marathon for a while. Nice place, with friendly people. I wound up having to take refuge deep in the Everglades during a hurricane with some new friends."

"Sounds very exciting," Charity said.

"What about you? Where are you headed after Key Biscayne?"

"The friends I'm picking up are accompanying me to the Bahamas for a few weeks."

Just then, Savannah's daughter returned with a bucket full of clams, joining them on the fly bridge. A beautiful little girl, Charity realized she'd misjudged her age. She was tall already, but only about seven or eight years old, with sandy brown hair and a deep tan. Like her mother, she was barefoot.

"Will you join us for dinner, Gabby?" Savannah asked. "Nothing special, just grunts and clams."

"Thanks, but I've already eaten," Charity lied. "I was planning to go to bed as soon as I got into the harbor, to catch the morning tide."

The three of them climbed down to the dock and said their goodbyes, before Charity returned to her own boat. As she started down into the cabin, she waved at the two of them, thinking that the little girl looked vaguely familiar.

Back aboard the *Dancer*, Charity sat down at the nav station and switched on the batteries. Though she'd been using some of the electronics, automated winches, and both the FM and weather radios during the crossing, the batteries still showed fully charged. Besides the gen-set, there were several small solar panels on the cabin roof and a wind generator aft the cockpit on a short mast. They'd produced enough electricity to keep the batteries charged during the short two-hour crossing.

She switched on the air conditioner, even though she knew the interior would rarely get hot. The waterline outside the hull was several feet above the cabin sole, and she remembered her uncle's boat staying cool in the summer and warm in the winter, just from the surrounding water.

With the air conditioner humming quietly, she went around the salon and galley, turning on every light and appliance. She wanted to make sure the auto-switch turned on the gen-set before the batteries drained too low. The boat's house load was on four deep-cycle marine batteries, with two separate batteries for the engine, one a backup. All six batteries were charged through the gen-set, the alternator on the diesel engine, or the solar panels and wind turbine.

Going to the entertainment center on the forward bulkhead of the salon, she knelt and opened the CD cabinet. Choosing an old Coltrane CD, she inserted it into the stereo.

With the volume turned low, soft jazz emanated from half a dozen speakers located throughout the salon. Charity released the catch that allowed the slotted CD holder to swing out. Behind it was a plain black tactical rifle case. She pulled the heavy case out and placed it on the settee table, folding up both sides for additional room and support.

Opening the case, she first removed the Leupold scope and set it aside. She'd been training with this very rifle and scope for several months and knew the ATN night optics had a fresh battery installed and the Mark 4 scope was zeroed in at five hundred yards. Shorter than that, the trajectory was nearly flat, and beyond that it dropped very little to a thousand yards. The heavy weapon had an effective range of over a mile. Though she'd become very adept at employing the weapon, her skills still hadn't matched its ability. But she was comfortable at a thousand yards.

Her rifle of choice was the new Barrett M82A1A, designed specifically to fire either a standard fifty-caliber BMG round or the Raufoss-manufactured Mk 211 incendiary round.

Director Stockwell had cautioned her that the round was intended for use against heavily-armored vehicles. She'd told him that she'd keep that in mind, but she knew that if she found an occasion with multiple terrorists grouped close together, a single round, fired into a man's chest, could kill several others nearby.

In Charity Styles's mind, there was only one way to deal with radical terrorists. Kill them. Better still if they became dead while vaporizing into many pieces. Gingerly, almost lovingly, she began to disassemble the rifle, knowing full well that it was already spotless.

CHAPTER EIGHT:

After the training exercise that morning, Awad Qureshi joined the others as the group gathered for lunch in the shade of the large boulders. While they ate, Hussein walked among them, talking to each man in turn, dispensing advice, praise, or admonition.

Awad sat with Majdi, slightly away from the others. This was done at Hussein's direction. He felt the three leaders had to be separate but still a part of the group of fighters.

Finally, Hussein dipped into the cauldron for his portion of the midday stew and joined Awad and Majdi. "It was a good training session this morning. I think we can cut back on shooting practice to just once a day now."

Majdi looked up at the leader. "Do you think that wise? Some of these men still can't even hit the target."

Fire flickered behind Hussein's dark eyes. He didn't like his orders or comments to be questioned in the least. Only Majdi dared do so, and then only on the subject of marksmanship. During his years in Texas, he'd joined a hunting club and was very proficient with a rifle.

"Our targets in San Antonio will be larger and closer," Hussein said. "And we will be firing on full automatic. But, if one or two of the men still needs training, you may work with them."

"I will," Majdi said and returned to eating his stew.

Hussein watched him, his eyes still smoldering slightly. Awad pretended to be engrossed in his meal, but noted Hussein's attitude and Majdi's indifference.

Hussein glanced quickly at Awad, catching his eye for a moment. A calmness replaced the fire in the leader's eyes. He spoke to Majdi as he watched Awad. "We depart this mountain in ten days, Majdi. Do what you can with them."

The leader stood quickly and tossed the remnants of his stew on the ground for the foraging night animals then disappeared up the trail to the rim of the volcano.

"You shouldn't antagonize him," Awad said. "He is like the lynx, very unpredictable."

Majdi looked up at his friend and whispered, "He is a fool. His rash actions may bring failure to our mission before we kill more than a handful of the infidels. Ten more days is simply not adequate."

Awad went back to eating his stew and thinking. Part of what Majdi said was true. In the early days of the current war with the infidels, the name Hussein Seif al Din Asfour had been known all across the northern provinces. Yes, his actions then could be seen as rash, even reckless. But he had been known as a fighter who gave no quarter, nor asked any, and always came out on top.

Right up until he was wounded and captured by the American Army.

Awad prided himself on his intellect, and Majdi, though only an engine mechanic, was wiser than he. Majdi never did anything fast. Some saw him as lazy, but Awad knew that every movement the man made, no matter how insignificant, was calculated and thought out well in advance.

Majdi spoke to Awad of his engines from time to time, whenever he was bored. How simply, yet perfectly, all the parts worked together for a common purpose—but only if they were assembled correctly and meticulously, he'd said.

Awad could see in his mind exactly what his friend meant, in comparing his engines to this group. Awad knew next to nothing about machinery. He'd get into his car, turn the key, and the machinery worked or it didn't.

Football was Awad's passion. Not the wild and deranged sport Americans called football, but the game he'd played in college. Moving his teammates down the field, with nothing more than a glance. Passing the ball with the side of his foot to another player, while making the opposing team think he was doing something else.

Yes, football was akin to Majdi's engines. Working together toward the goal and victorious if the right parts were assembled in the right order with precision.

Looking around at the other men in the group, Awad wondered if any played football, if they could be directed and guided with little more than a glance or nod.

He would talk to Hussein about football later tonight. He knew the man had played while in the American prison in Cuba. He'd spoken of it to Awad, when Hussein had learned that Awad had been the team's captain at his college. Perhaps he could plant a seed in the leader's mind—cause him to think ahead like Majdi and himself.

CHAPTER NINE:

The soft patter of rain on the roof of the cabin roof woke Charity. She'd slept soundly, curled up in the forward vee-berth. No nightmares. As she lay on the bunk, looking at the heavy timbers in the overhead, her mind drifted back, recalling the familiar surroundings from her childhood.

She felt as if this boat could protect her from the recurring dreams, certain that these strong oak ribs and cross members, identical to those she had traced with her hands as a little girl, held some mystical and all-powerful quality that would see no harm come to her.

But it was the horrible images that came to her in the night that fueled her. The doctors had deemed her mentally unfit to return to flight duty status after her capture and two days of being raped and tortured. She'd been completely open and forthright with the Army's shrinks. In retrospect, she probably shouldn't have been.

Reaching a hand out, Charity touched one of the heavy timbers. In her mind's eye, the hand was that of a ten-year-old girl, tentative and shy. A familiar shape and texture. Nearly everything about this boat—the look, the lines, the way she handled—was both intimately familiar and, at the same time, distantly strange.

Rising from the bunk, she went aft to the galley and turned the coffeemaker on. She'd set it up the night before. Quickly, she brushed her teeth at the galley sink before going forward to the head for a shower while the coffee brewed.

Space was a constant problem aboard any kind of boat. The *Dancer's* head was only three feet square and included the marine toilet and shower. The only sink was in the galley. The shower had four waterproof switches, two for the seawater pumps and two more for the pumps that supplied the precious fresh water. The heating elements for the hot water switches were in the pipes themselves. There was no hot water storage tank. The heating elements produced very hot water, though.

Flipping the switch for hot seawater to the on position, Charity waited until the automatic pump began to hum. When steaming hot water jetted out of the shower head mounted to the overhead, Charity sat down on the toilet and let the hot water cascade over her for a moment before picking up the soap and scrub brush. After ten minutes, she turned the seawater switch off and flicked on the cold fresh water to quickly rinse off. The fresh water tank only held a hundred gallons. There was plenty of bottled water on board, so fresh drinking water wouldn't be a problem.

Stepping out of the shower, her skin red and raw from the stiff bristles of the brush, she opened the hanging closet directly opposite the head and chose a pair of light-weight khaki pants and a light blue long-sleeved denim shirt. She'd be in the sun all day, if the rain quit.

Toweling off and dressing in the salon, she then went forward and made the bunk, switching on the VHF weather forecast. The local frequency's monotone electronic voice, identical to most others along the coast, told her that a passing shower would dissipate by midmorning.

At the nav station, she opened the laptop. While it was booting up, she took a banana from one of the baskets and poured a mug of steaming hot coffee. She ate quickly and sat down at the desk to drink her coffee and check her email for any change in the status of her target. It was time to begin the hunt.

Every day, sometimes several times a day, Director Stockwell had told her, an encrypted email would be written on an anonymous server. The email wouldn't be sent. Instead, it would be saved as a draft by the sender, an unknown analyst in the bowels of the Pentagon. Charity had access to the server and could then read the email in the draft file and delete it. Simple, yet this effectively left no electronic trail. She could also respond to it and ask for more information, assistance, or request additional gear, then save the request again as a draft.

If Charity needed additional equipment, it would be supplied at sea. Director Stockwell had been adamant about this. Between all the intelligence agencies and the military, someone was flying somewhere over the Caribbean just about every day. A location for a drop would be arranged, and whatever she asked for would be dropped in a buoyant watertight package, with a VHF beacon that would bring her right to it. Charity didn't anticipate needing anything more than her rifle on this mission.

With no update, she plotted her course on the laptop, which would feed information to the helm, including the direction and speed of surface winds and currents, and could sail the *Dancer* all by itself if need be. A valuable tool to be able to sail solo through the nights ahead.

Her destination was the Gulf Coast of Mexico, a small town called Alvarado, not far from Veracruz and west of the Yucatan Peninsula. The plotter calculated the sailing distance as just over nine hundred and seventy nautical miles. If she could maintain a six-knot average, she'd arrive there in six days.

Charity started the boat's engine and, grabbing the damp towel to dry the seat at the helm, she went out into the rain and raised the Bimini top over the cockpit. It didn't really afford much protection from a driving rain, but the wind was very light right now, and the misty rain was falling straight down. NOAA was predicting the wind would build to fifteen knots out of the east shortly after sunrise, and heavier rain would fall before the weather dissipated and she should have light to moderate seas outside the safety of Biscayne Bay.

Stepping over to the dock, she untied the lines, standing on the dock and holding them for a moment. *Sea Biscuit* was dark, Savannah and her daughter still asleep. Charity looked around the small harbor and the little island. This would be her last time on dry land for nearly a week and her last time on American soil for quite some time. A feeling of uncertainty swept over her. She was a confident sailor and already knew *Wind Dancer* in so many ways. Yet the trepidation she felt persisted.

Shaking it off, Charity grabbed the rail and gave the boat a slight shove away from the seawall, stepping aboard and securing the lines. She moved quickly to the helm, flipping the switch to open the doors for the bow thruster. A moment later, she had the boat aimed at the channel and engaged the transmission, while watching the sonar. It showed more than eight feet of water ahead as she steered the big sailboat into the channel.

Clearing the point where the pavilion was located, Charity turned *Wind Dancer* south, following the seawall, just thirty feet to port. The VHF radio crackled, startling her. "*Sea Biscuit* calling *Wind Dancer.*"

"Go to channel seventy-two, *Sea Biscuit,*" Charity said into the microphone.

She switched frequencies and waited a moment, then Savannah's voice came over the radio. "I wasn't sure if you were going to head out in this soup, Gabby."

"It should clear by the time I reach Key Biscayne," she replied. "I thought I'd go ahead and get my sea legs ready before getting there, so I'm running on the outside."

"How many friends are you picking up?"

Charity wondered if she was just making idle conversation or if the question was something else. Deciding that her training had made her paranoid about anyone outside her old team, she replied, "Just three. A couple and their friend, a young man who we will be dropping off in Nassau to work."

A hearty laugh came over the speaker. "Girl, you've been set up. Your friends are playing matchmaker."

Charity grinned as she turned into the cut on the south side of Boca Chita Key and glanced down at the sonar screen. Twelve feet and no obstructions. She nudged the throttle slightly, and the *Dancer* slowly picked up speed. She decided that she liked this independent-minded woman and pretended to play out the fantasy.

"Well, the man will be in for a rude awakening if he's looking for any kind of commitment. A roll in a hammock, maybe, but that's it."

Savannah laughed again. They talked for a few minutes, as the *Dancer* moved through the channel and into the wide-open Atlantic Ocean, the bow cleaving the small swells with little change in the attitude of the boat. The rain continued to fall lightly on the Bimini as the first shades of purple started to brighten the eastern sky ahead.

The wind was out of the east, and the *Dancer* was headed straight into it. Still too light a breeze for sailing, though. Knowing that Savannah was likely on her fly bridge, Charity held the easterly course until she was three miles offshore, while they chatted about places they'd been.

"I have a feeling we'll see one another again," Savannah said.

"That would be nice, Savannah. Next time, the beer's on me."

"Fair winds and following seas, *Wind Dancer*. *Sea Biscuit* out and back to sixteen."

Continuing due east, the rain began to fall a little harder and the wind was picking up. The Bimini covered the entire cockpit and part of the cabin roof. If the rain became too heavy, she had a clear plastic dodger that attached to the forward edge of the Bimini and the cab-in roof ahead of the hatch. It extended down both sides, halfway encompassing the cockpit. The helm, however, was open aft and to the sides.

After another ten minutes, the rain just stopped. No lightening, no slowing, it just ended, as if it had never been raining. Ahead, the first faint rays of sunshine were beginning to dim the few stars she could see near the horizon. Charity looked aft and could just see the patter of rain on the surface, retreating in her wake.

Still within cell tower range, she took her phone out and pulled up the Weather Channel website. The weather radar map told her that she was clear of the rain, and from what she could tell by zooming out, the day was going to be bright and sunny.

The small surface radar image on the console showed her she was nearly alone on the ocean. Only a few ships further out and some smaller vessels closer to shore, probably fishing boats.

Charity activated the automatic winches, raising the mainsail, then unfurled the jib, hauling it back to the starboard side, all without having to leave the helm. The sails luffed in the light wind, the bow aimed straight into it.

She cut the engine and turned the wheel slightly to starboard. *Wind Dancer* responded slowly and lost a little speed. Then Charity heard and felt the familiar snap of the sails. The light wind filled them, sending a tingle through her spine and up her neck. The big boat heeled slightly, and she experienced the same rush of excitement she always felt when the wind filled her sails.

As the sun climbed higher, Charity steered more southerly, angling away from shore into deeper water. Once she was pointed due south, she activated the winch control for the forestay, adding thirty percent more canvas area to capture the wind.

Dancer responded better than Charity had hoped, heeling further and accelerating. The computer display on the console told her she had a ten-knot wind directly out of the east, and the boat was clipping along at nearly eight knots on the small swells, taking them on the port beam.

As the boat's forward speed increased, the apparent direction of the wind changed, pointing higher. She activated the winches, hauling the boom and foresails in closer. *Dancer* quickly reached that perfect equilibrium, using forward speed to increase both the apparent wind speed and direction. Glancing at the knot meter, she was amazed that *Dancer* was skimming along at nine knots, heeled over only ten degrees.

As the day wore on, Charity began to turn more and more westerly, following the curve of the Florida Keys, staying between the chain of islands and the great Gulf Stream to the south. The Stream flowed east through the Florida Straits, then north up the Atlantic Seaboard. Sailing in its current would cut her speed drastically.

At noon, she set the autopilot and engaged the computer's winch controls, allowing the boat to find its most optimal course and sail arrangement. The winches whined, moving the sails in and out, until the computer was satisfied.

Charity checked the knot meter and saw that the boat's speed hadn't changed all that much, over what she had done manually. This gave her a small sense of satisfaction. It'd been some time since she'd sailed a boat of this size. For the last few years, she'd been keeping her skills sharp, sailing a much smaller twenty-four-foot San Juan sloop.

Checking the radar once again and seeing nothing ahead, she went down to the galley to make lunch. She quickly threw together a sandwich and took the ripest mango from one of the nets, cutting it into thin slices before returning to the cockpit.

This is going to be my life for the next few days, she thought, sitting back down at the helm and placing her plate beside her. All day and all night at the helm, with few breaks, sleeping right here for an hour or two while letting the computer sail the *Dancer*.

The more westerly her course became, following the sweep of the Keys, the broader the reach of the sails. Though the wind was holding at fifteen knots, by midafternoon, her forward speed had dropped to just seven knots, running before the wind.

Late afternoon found her just off Key West. Beginning to doubt her ability to sail straight on through the night, catnapping at the helm, for five days, she decided to take advantage of the last anchorage before crossing the southern part of the Gulf of Mexico, the Dry Tortugas. In November, there probably wouldn't be anyone else at the old fort sixty miles west of Key West. If there was, she'd anchor outside the harbor on the lee side of the Fort Jefferson ruins.

Approaching the old fort just after ten o'clock, with the moon directly overhead and slightly astern, she couldn't see any boats in the anchorage. Relieved, she started the engine and furled the sails. Thirty minutes later, after circling around to the north approach, *Wind Dancer* motored sedately into Bird Key Harbor. Charity chose this spot over the more popular anchorage on the east side of the fort, just in case another boat arrived during the night.

After the anchor dropped with a splash and Charity killed the engine, the silence of the night was overwhelming. Only the slightest sound of the tiny ripples in the harbor tickling the hull could be heard.

"Yeah," she said aloud, breaking the stillness of the night. "I'll get a good night's sleep and start fresh tomorrow."

It wasn't in Charity Styles's nature to second-guess her decisions. But, throughout the day, the ocean seemed to get larger and larger and the boat smaller and smaller. She'd covered two hundred miles of ocean in nineteen hours.

Only eight hundred more to go, she thought. Even at seven knots, she could cover that in five more days.

"What's an extra day?" she said aloud, talking to herself again. A gull on Bird Key Bank answered her, its laughing cry punctuating the doubt she was feeling.

"Fuck you," she shouted to the anonymous gull. "Bet you'll never see the Mexican coast."

Double-checking the anchor, Charity went below, closing and securing the hatch for the night. She'd eaten an hour earlier and wasn't hungry, so she took a quick shower under the cold fresh water, just to get the salt off her skin. It was a luxury she probably couldn't indulge in while underway.

After getting ready for bed, she changed her mind and decided to unwind a little on deck before going to sleep. She grabbed her hammock from a storage bin and a cold beer from the fridge, and went back up on deck. Securing one end of the hammock to the mast and the other end to an eye ring in the lower part of the boom, she tested it with her hands.

Satisfied, Charity stretched out in the hammock, the light breeze cool on her skin, causing goosebumps wherever it touched. The first long pull from the cold beer tasted good, so she took another, marveling at how many stars she could see. A meteor streaked across the western sky, behind the *Dancer*, and she made a little-girl's wish on it.

No television program could match nature's show, she thought, before exhaustion overtook her and she fell asleep.

CHAPTER TEN:

The nightmares came while Charity slept out in the open. The dank dinginess of the cave where she'd been held captive in Afghanistan, the putrid smell of garbage and human waste.

Charity's head shook from side to side as she slept. Behind her clenched eyes, the shadows of several men moved through the gloom around her, each man laughing and taking his turn with her body. The pain of rough entry and the sickly smell of the men grunting above her, as she was bent over and tied to a table, had nearly made her sick. She'd remained in that position for more than a day, as at least a dozen men had beaten raped, and sodomized her, over and over.

They had taken her twelve times that first hour. After bending her over and tying her to the table, they'd sliced her trousers across the back and down both legs with a razor-sharp knife, leaving deep cuts in her skin. The rest of her trousers had been literally ripped from her body in the men's frenzied lust, leaving only the top portion and her belt.

As the men had used her lower body for their sadistic pleasure, they'd used her upper body and face for a punching bag, moving around the table and taking turns raping and beating her, without mercy. A coarsely braided rope had stung her back each time she'd tried to move. The man swinging it would roar with laughter when the thick rope had torn at her shirt and skin, leaving both in tatters.

In her mind, as she tossed and turned in the hammock, Charity saw the man's face looming above her. He'd grabbed her by the hair and twisted her head around so he could spit in her battered and bleeding face. He was the leader of the group, and two days after her capture, he had been the one guarding her when the attack had come. He had been the only one in the cave with Charity when she'd managed to free herself in the confusion of the attack. He'd had his back to her, absorbed in the madness of battle outside the cave.

She'd somehow managed to find the knife the leader had used to slice her trousers off. It'd been tossed into the recesses of the cave, covered with sand, when she'd struggled against them each time they came for their daily rape sessions.

Charity had been tossed into the recesses of the cave as well, fed occasional scraps and given tepid water if she begged for it. Her captors found that particularly amusing. They'd all but forget about her, until their base animal urges needed release. She had found the knife on the morning of her third day in captivity.

Charity had quietly slipped up behind the Taliban leader, wearing only her boots, the remnants of her uniform top, ripped open in the back, and her belt, which held up a ragged portion of her uniform trousers like a loincloth. She'd stumbled at first, when getting up. She'd felt weak and feverish.

With her left hand, she'd grabbed the leader from behind, her hand over his mouth, then plunged the blade deep into his back, thrusting upward and twisting the knife with all her might. The knife was sharp and well made. The backward-curved bolster had kept her hand from slipping off the handle as the man's blood spilled over the knife's handle, leaving it slick in her clenched fist.

The man had dropped to his knees then, as Charity yanked the blade out. She'd then yanked his head back by the hair, dragging him down onto his back in the filth of the cave. Kneeling over him, still holding him by his hair, she'd bent low over his face, staring at him fiercely through one eye, the other swollen shut.

The malevolence and hatred she'd seen in his eyes was gone then. All she could see in his dark eyes was fear. They'd blinked rapidly, pink foam dribbling from the corner of his mouth. The man's life was coming to an end quickly.

Charity hacked phlegm into her mouth and spat in his face before plunging the long blade upward into his chest. She'd pushed the knife up from below the rib cage and yanked it from side to side, shredding the man's black heart. All the while, she'd leaned close to his face, only inches away. She'd watched him closely as he died.

Watched as the fear left his eyes and they simply went blank, like two lumps of coal.

Charity's eyes snapped open and she stared up into the predawn sky, blinking. The moon was near the western horizon, the light from it reflecting off the shimmering surface of the Gulf of Mexico, like a million diamonds on a carpet of black velvet.

She swung her legs out of the hammock and placed them on the cabin roof, solid and comforting. The psychologists had prescribed drugs, counseling, meditation, and dozens of other things to keep the dreams at bay.

During her rehab in Israel, she'd met an Israeli soldier who'd spent four months as a prisoner. He'd told her how to use her dreams. "Don't fight them. Use them to fight," he'd told her. Physically healed, she'd followed her new friend's advice, participating in months of hand-to-hand fight training.

She'd learned the basics of the Israeli combat technique known as Krav Maga. Unlike the eastern martial arts, there was nothing fluid, graceful, or self-defensive about Krav Maga. She learned to incapacitate and kill viciously and efficiently, using knives, rocks, even her bare hands. Whatever was handy could be used as a weapon to overcome violence with greater and more focused violence.

Standing, Charity felt a sudden wave of resolve wash over her body. No longer uncertain, she was ready to move on with a single-minded tenacity. The dreams fueled her for the fight.

Changing into sailing clothes in the salon, she started the engine before sitting down to check her email. There was only one message. Her target was still in place, encamped with more than a dozen other terrorists. They were still training in the crater of the extinct volcano, with their camp somewhere on the densely forested southern slope. They hadn't moved in two days, but she would need to hurry. The information had been gleaned by a satellite circling high in space, looking down with its powerful camera arrays.

Checking the weather for the southern Gulf, between the Tortugas and the Yucatan, she was assured of good strong winds and a light following sea.

The port city of Progresso, on the northern tip of the Yucatan Peninsula, lay only thirty miles off the direct course to Alvarado. From her current location, a course change of only a couple degrees would allow her to clear customs there. It would be a four-hundred-and-thirty-nautical-mile trip to reach it, then another three hundred and eighty miles to Alvarado. But getting her visa stamped far from where she would kill someone seemed like a good idea.

Updating her course plotter, with Progresso as a way-point, Charity figured that if the *Dancer* could average seven knots, she'd arrive in the Yucatan seaport before dusk in a little over two days. She could decide as she neared the Yucatan whether to clear customs there and lay over for another night, or press on to her objective in Alvarado.

The low whine of the electric windlass as it hauled up the anchor line was the only sound in the harbor, save for the quiet burble of the diesel engine's exhaust. Both were drowned out when the first part of the twenty-foot anchor chain clattered over the pulley. Charity shifted to neutral until the anchor seated itself, to keep it from swinging into the hull. She then put the transmission back into gear, and *Wind Dancer* moved slowly through the harbor toward open water.

The rattling anchor chain must have awakened the gulls, and they took to flight from their perches on the nearby mangroves. Wheeling and crying angrily at the intrusion on their slumber, the birds punctuated the silence of the predawn hour with a cacophony of noise. It reminded Charity of the fake laugh track used in old sitcoms.

Clear of the markers, Charity turned south and raised the sails to the steady easterly breeze. They nagged and grabbed at the breeze as they unfurled, slowly heeling the *Dancer* to starboard a little at a time. Shutting the engine off, Charity made a slow, sweeping turn to the southwest, allowing the computer to control the reach of the sails. Pointing the bow toward the setting moon, the computer reached out with the boom and foresails to capture as much wind as possible.

A quick glance at the screen told her the wind was at nine knots and her forward speed only six. But she knew that once the sun rose and the far shores warmed, the easterly trade wind would increase.

She'd brought the file up with her. Once she reached deeper water, Charity engaged the autopilot only a mile from the tiny anchorage. By the light of a small headlamp, she opened the file and again studied the face of the man she was going to kill. Hussein Seif al Din Asfour was evil and deserved a slower death than her rifle would allow.

In the Gitmo photo, his beard was thin, like that of a much younger man. The barely existent mustache didn't even connect to the sparse hairs on his cheeks. Below his cruel-looking mouth, there was only a patch in the center, his face bare to mid chin on either side of it. His hair had the typical Gitmo style, buzz cut to a fraction of an inch, receding slightly on the sides of a narrow forehead. Eyes darkly evil looking, with bushy eyebrows.

Flipping the page, she read the reports from eyewitnesses all across northern Afghanistan, who had him killing anyone who stood in his path before his capture. He and his men had tortured, raped, and killed women and little girls with apparent impunity. Everyone in the northern provinces feared him, including the authorities. Everywhere he'd gone, fear preceded his arrival and mourning followed his departure.

Subsequent pages expanded on the atrocities he'd committed, in the cold, analytical prose of government spooks. Charity emotionlessly read each one again, the words echoing in her mind, filling her subconscious with revulsion. Her conscious mind, however, steeled itself with a resolve so strong it buried the other thoughts.

This man must die, she thought. *Die like the guard in the cave, cold metal ripping through his evil heart.*

An hour later, as the *Dancer* approached the edge of the Gulf Stream, Charity disconnected the autopilot and turned due south, hauling the sheets in to gain speed and cross the strong current as quickly as possible.

Wind Dancer responded, gathering speed, the wind now up to twelve knots, as Charity activated the three winches and brought the sails in close-hauled. *Dancer* surged forward to nine knots.

She felt the strong pull of the current, as the bow crossed into the Stream. With the water trying to move the boat east, against the wind, and *Dancer* pointing south, she heeled more sharply, like a draft horse leaning into the harness to pull up a stubborn tree stump.

Dancer didn't falter or stumble, but charged ahead as if she wanted to get shed of the bonds the current held on her. The spray from the wind and current-driven waves flew off the port bow and back across the side deck.

Charity stood up, gripping the handles of the antique ship's wheel with both hands. Salty spray blew against her, dampening her shirt, face, and hair, as *Wind Dancer* cleaved each wave. The exhilaration she felt brought a slight grin to her face as the wind tugged at her clothes and hair.

It only took twenty minutes to cross the narrow current, and Charity relished every minute of it. Finally, she turned back to her original southwesterly heading, reengaging the autopilot. The computer made a slight course correction and adjustment of the sails, bound once more for the Yucatan.

The day wore on. Once the sun rose higher, the wind became steady at fifteen knots. *Dancer* held her course, pushing steadily toward the southwest. The computer constantly made minute changes in the sail arrangement, keeping her speed a steady six to seven knots.

Charity went below after checking the radar. Moving quickly through the salon, she stripped off her damp, salt-crusted clothes, tossing them on the cabin sole, by the hatch to the forward berth.

After a cold freshwater shower, she stepped out into the companionway and got a clean pair of pants and a shirt from the hanging closet, a bra and panties from a drawer. She rolled them up tightly together and left the roll on the forward berth. Then she took a white bikini out of the drawer and quickly put it on. She wanted to take advantage of the bright morning sunlight. An hour each day under the heat of the tropical sun would darken her already deep tan. With her hair now black, she should be able to pass for a local quite easily.

Back at the helm, Charity pulled her hair straight back from her forehead, securing it high on the back of her head with an elastic band she had on her wrist.

Stretching out on the starboard bench seat, she then read and reread the information in the file again. Every detail of the man's atrocities against the people of Afghanistan, every crease and pore in the skin of his face, she memorized.

At noon, Charity checked the radar screen and, seeing nothing near her, she went forward along the port deck. Checking equipment and rigging, she unclipped her safety line, moving it to each new section of the rail as she went. The belt was uncomfortable around her bare midsection, but very necessary.

Her uncle had survived hypothermia after a full day in the water when a rogue wave had hit his boat and he'd fallen overboard. He always insisted that a safety line should always be used while moving around above deck on a boat that was underway.

Out here, there'd be almost no chance of rescue, as the computer would continue to sail the boat to Mexico without her, leaving her in the middle of the vast ocean, the nearest land many miles away to the south. *Wind Dancer* was now closer to Cuba than to the United States, the communist country stretching away to the southwest, the coastline roughly paralleling her course, only about fifty miles away...

Reaching the bow, she double-checked the seating of the large Danforth anchor. Satisfied, she paused for a moment, standing on the pitching deck at the forward-most part of the boat, the giant foresail and jib behind her. The bow moved left and right with the wave action, as *Dancer* rode up the back of one small swell after another. A few clouds could be seen far away to the south-southwest, over the western tip of Cuba, but ahead of her, the sky was clear and cobalt blue. Perfect sailing weather.

Back at the helm, she put the Bimini back up, checked the radar screen again, and then went below to make lunch and change clothes. As she was about to climb back up the ladder to the cockpit, the laptop at the nav station pinged an alert for a saved message, and she sat down to open it.

The anonymous sender advised her that recent chatter among known Hezbollah members had mentioned an attack in Texas in less than ten days. The Hezbollah cell mentioned was currently somewhere in Mexico.

Ten days, she thought, munching on an apple. *Not much time.*

If she stopped in Progresso, even for only the night, that meant she'd have only three days after arriving in Alvarado to acquire transportation to the interior and scout out the terrorists' location, then come up with some way to get close enough to take out the leader and still get back out.

Deleting the message, she created a new one to save in the draft folder.

Please advise with utmost expedience any further chatter involving this attack threat and any update on the group currently camped at the San Martin Tuxtla volcano.

Taking her lunch and three more bottles of water, Charity returned to the helm. She ate slowly, reading the file for at least the sixth time, only occasionally looking forward or checking the radar. The system had an alarm that would warn her of any boat traffic within two miles, plenty of time to disengage the autopilot and take evasive action. It would come in handy during the night, when she'd sleep in hour-long intervals at the helm.

Fourteen hours after leaving the Dry Tortugas, with the sun sinking slowly toward the horizon directly ahead, *Wind Dancer* had covered a hundred and twenty miles of ocean. The sun turned a russet shade of red, bathing the clouds to the south in pastel hues of pink and lavender.

Charity had actually cooked a hot meal an hour earlier. The seas were so calm, she had no trouble broiling a chicken breast with sautéed onions and sliced potatoes. Standing on the ladder to the cockpit, she could see all around the *Dancer* and keep watch on the food as it sizzled. While it wasn't a four-star meal, she didn't think it half bad and allowed herself a single bottle of beer afterward. Just to celebrate the end of the day.

The sun, red and enormous, began its daily dance with the sea. At the same time, the moon began to rise behind *Wind Dancer*, presenting its own beautiful shade of red. The two pirouetted together, one setting, the other rising at the same pace, moving in a surreal dance of light that gave greater depth and texture to the water's surface and *Dancer* herself. Light played across the bow and sails, bathing them in the warmth of a sun and giving everything it touched a strange sort of enigmatic power. The sun itself appeared larger than usual, as if Charity could almost reach out and touch it.

Suddenly, it looked as if the water just reached up and grabbed the huge red disc. Charity gasped lightly as she saw this, her breath catching in her throat, and for a moment it was so beautiful she thought she would cry.

The water continued pulling at the sun, grasping ever upward at the sides, seeming to stretch it horizontally. The sun flattened itself along the horizon, as if resisting the steady pull of the sea.

In just a few minutes, as Charity watched the display in awe, the water's surface finally reached over the top of the sun, embracing the last of it and pulling it down as a small inverted teardrop, bright orange against the purple sky, escaped its grasp. The teardrop leaped from the sea, hovering just above the horizon for an instant, before it blinked out and darkness fell over the water.

Within a minute, the purple light in the west disappeared and stars twinkled all across the sky, right down to the horizon. Dusk in the open sea was nonexistent. Day turned into night in the blink of an eye.

With the light of the moon behind her, the stars shining everywhere she looked, Charity was again reminded just how small and insignificant one person, even one boat, really is in the vastness of Earth's ocean. Her eyes adjusted quickly, as the last light from the sun faded and disappeared. By the light of the nearly full moon and the billions of stars reflecting in her eyes, she could easily see for miles out across the empty ocean.

The automatic lighting system turned on the running lights, casting an eerie green-and-red glow on the water on either side of the bow. *Dancer* seemed not to notice the change, but sailed steadfastly onward.

Rising, Charity went below to put the file away and check for an update. With nothing in her draft folder, she went to the hanging closet and put on a sweater against the chilly night air. She also picked up one of the water-resistant pillows from the settee and carried it to the cockpit.

It would now be nearly eleven hours of darkness before the first rays of the sun would snatch the darkness away from night, just as quickly as a lamp being turned on.

Back at the helm, alone with her thoughts, Charity thought about her friends, the members of her team. The people she'd been training with, some of them for over a year. She hoped that one day, the truth about her disappearance would be told. She didn't know why it mattered, but it was important to her that these people knew why she'd left them.

In particular, she hoped her boss, Deuce Livingston, would be told and that he'd understand. Charity respected his quiet leadership. She knew Andrew would understand. If and when he learned the truth, he'd laugh, and with that deep foghorn voice of his, he'd proclaim that he had known better all along.

Jesse McDermitt, the team's part-time transporter and close friend of both Deuce and his father before him, would certainly understand. After twenty years in the Marines, he'd gone to the Keys to escape everything. On his wedding day, a year and a half ago, his bride had been kidnapped and murdered by people involved in bringing terrorists into the country. Charity said a silent prayer that life would bring peace to the man.

As the night wore on, Charity became tired. She planned to sleep one hour on and one hour off, from ten to an hour after sunrise. Tomorrow night would be more difficult. She planned to take at least an hour's nap after lunch, then start her hour-long naps as soon as she started feeling drowsy.

Setting the alarm on her watch to sound in an hour and then repeat every two hours after that, Charity curled up in the corner of the starboard bench, making sure to shorten her safety line and attach it to the eye hook on the side of the console.

Her conscious mind tried to fight sleep. It wasn't natural for her to sleep while moving. She'd always had trouble doing it in a car when someone else was driving.

She finally convinced herself that there wasn't anything within the twelve-mile limit of the radar, and it would alert her if another boat was close. Besides, in an hour, *Dancer* would only travel seven or eight miles. Exhausted, she fell asleep.

It only felt like a minute or two passed before the alarm on Charity's watch sounded. She hadn't slept long enough to enter the dream state, and she awakened sluggishly.

Checking the radar and plotter, she saw that she'd actually traveled nearly seven miles from the location she had checked just before lying down. The radar screen still revealed an empty ocean, nothing within twelve miles. Beyond its range, a fleet of mega tankers could be bearing down on her, but due to the curvature of the Earth, neither her eyes, nor the radar could see them.

As the *Dancer* rode up the back of the slower-moving little swells, then settled deep into the trough, the steady swish of the bow wave was hypnotic. The steady rhythm soon lulled her into closing her eyes again.

Snapping her head up, Charity checked her watch and position. This time, it really had only been minutes. She kept her mind busy, checking the distance to Progresso and calculating in her head how long it would take to get there.

At eleven thirty, she went below to get a couple of oranges to snack on later. Leaving them in the cockpit, she clipped her safety line to the cable on the port side and went forward, inspecting the rigging and gear.

At the bow, she stood motionless a moment, as was becoming her habit, and looked out beyond the *Wind Dancer* to the horizon. The moon had passed its zenith and was now slightly ahead of her as they both raced toward the coast of Mexico. Somewhere over the horizon was a man who only had a week or so to live, but didn't know it.

The small swells throughout the day had diminished to occasional ripples, the nearby water's surface shimmering with the moon's reflection. The only sound was the now-constant swish of the bow, cutting through the water at a steady seven knots.

By midnight, *Wind Dancer* had covered just under two hundred miles since leaving the anchorage in the Dry Tortugas that morning. Charity checked her position, dropping a waypoint on the plotter again. It would tell her how far the boat had traveled when the alarm woke her again. This time, her conscious mind didn't fight it and Charity fell asleep almost instantly, curled up on the padded bench seat.

CHAPTER ELEVEN:

Shouts and excited voices woke Charity. She jumped to her feet, but the shortened tether caused her to stumble, and she went down to one knee on the deck.

A scraping sound brought her fully awake as more shouts, just over the port rail, filled the air. Charity quickly lengthened the safety line and stood up, flipping off the autopilot.

A woman screamed behind her in the darkness. Charity cursed to herself. *Dammit! I hit a boat.* Engaging the electric furling system, she quickly had the sails furled and started the engine, turning the *Dancer* around.

Charity took a powerful spotlight from under the bench and pointed it to where she thought the other boat should be. Scanning the water back and forth with the light, she finally saw it. But it wasn't a boat—at least, not any kind of boat she'd ever seen before.

Cuban refugees, she thought.

Approaching the derelict-looking raft, keeping it on the starboard side, she cast the light all around, looking for anyone that might have been flung overboard in the collision.

Not seeing anyone in the water, she called out to them in Spanish. "Are you alright? I did not see you."

To her surprise a woman answered. "Yes, we are not hurt, but our boat is sinking!"

"How many are you?" Charity shouted, reaching under the bench again and pushing against a portion of the deck at the bottom. The spring released, just as the file on the computer had said it would, and a small section lifted up slightly. Charity pulled it full open and withdrew a Colt .45-caliber handgun. Quickly, she ratcheted the slide, chambering a round.

"We are four," the woman shouted back as the *Dancer* slowly approached. "Myself, my little boy and my parents. Please hurry, we're sinking, and my mother and son do not swim!"

Thrusting the pistol into her pants behind her back, Charity pulled her shirt and sweater down over it. Steering closer to the raft, she saw that it was built out of long pipes of some kind, each about eight inches in diameter. They were lashed together, and it appeared the raft had a small engine mounted right in the middle, but it didn't sound like it was running.

The collision had severed the ropes binding the makeshift hull together. At the stern, the pipes on the port side were askance, hanging in the water, with the deck awash and their belongings about to slip into the sea. A dark-haired woman in jeans and a white long-sleeved blouse clutched a small child of about three or four. Behind her, an elderly couple cowered, hanging on to the sides.

Charity shut off the engine as the *Dancer* came alongside. She moved quickly to the rail at the front of the cockpit and unhooked the rail cable. Strapped to *Dancer's* cabin roof was a folding ladder that could be hung over the side. She grabbed it and placed it over the low gunwale.

"Hurry," Charity shouted as she used a grapple to pull the failing raft alongside. "Grab anything that will not float and climb up the ladder."

The old man moved to the ladder and helped a frail-looking woman climb up. He followed quickly, faster than most men his age could move. Halfway up, he turned on the steps and took his grandson from his daughter. Passing the crying boy to his wife, he scrambled briskly up the ladder and reached down to his daughter.

The daughter handed several containers and a suitcase up to the old man before grabbing the ladder and hauling herself up, just as the raft came completely apart. The engine and the section of deck it was attached to sank into the black abyss.

For the next thirty minutes, Charity maneuvered *Dancer* around the flotsam, while the younger Cuban woman used the grapple to hook belongings and pull them out of the water.

Finally, everything that could be salvaged was now dripping in a soggy pile on the cockpit deck and the cabin roof. Charity introduced herself, using the maiden name of her alias, Gabriela Ortiz. The young woman introduced herself as Isabella Villanueva. Her little boy was Roberto, and her parents were Alonzo and Rosina Montoya.

"You have saved my family," Isabella said. "Our motor quit running halfway through the day, and the raft was beginning to fall apart."

"Saved your life?" Charity asked in flawless Mexican Spanish. "I'm so sorry I hit you."

"You've been sent by the angels," the elderly man said. His hair was snowy white, skin a dark brown, with deep furrows in his brow and cheeks. Shorter than his daughter, he was slightly built, his hands gnarled and bent, probably from decades of pulling on fishing nets, Charity guessed.

"I built that raft myself," the old man said. "The crossing to America was only to take two days and a single night. I fear it would have fallen apart and the sea claimed us all before this night was through. Isabella told me that an angel would come and deliver us."

"Please," Charity said, "let us go into the cabin where it is warmer. I will make you something to eat."

Charity went down first and helped Isabella down with the boy clutching her neck. "There's a bunk forward," Charity said. "And blankets to keep the boy warm."

As Isabella carried the boy to bed, Charity helped her aging parents down the steep ladder. Standing on the cabin sole, the old man looked around, eyes wide with wonder. "*Santa Madre de Dios,*" he said in a hushed voice.

Charity beckoned toward the center-facing couches in the salon. "Please, sit."

As the old couple moved forward, the man gingerly traced his crooked fingers along the polished woodwork, marveling at it. He took his wife's hand in his own, helping her to a seat on the starboard side, then he turned slowly, taking it all in.

"I know this boat," he said in slow Spanish, his eyes sparkling. When they finally fell on Charity, he said, "I once sailed on a sloop designed by the legendary John Alden. It was a lifetime ago. Long before..." His voice trailed off as he made a movement with his hand meant to mimic the stroking of a long beard.

"*No está en Cuba, señor,*" Charity said. "It is alright to say his name."

"You are going west?" he asked, obviously concerned for his family.

"Yes, I am going to Mexico. It is where I was born, but I live in America now."

His head fell, and he sank onto the couch as Isabella came back into the salon. "Roberto fell into a deep sleep," she said.

Charity knew there was no choice. She couldn't have continued sailing on without picking these people up, and she couldn't continue on with them. She sat down at the nav station and plotted a course for Key West. The sudden sound of the winches unfurling the sails and the snap of the canvas as they filled brought the old man out of his gloom.

"There are others aboard?" Alonzo asked, bewildered.

"No," Charity replied. "*Wind Dancer* can sail herself."

Charity pulled up the radar display on the laptop and saw nothing to the northeast. She moved to the small galley, put a pot on the stove and opened three cans of vegetable soup. "I will take you part of the way to America," she said. "Close enough that you can get there on your own, using my dinghy."

The delay would cost her dearly and may cause her to fail in her mission. The alternative was to march these refugees up on deck and shoot them.

Isabella helped Charity prepare sandwiches, thanking her repeatedly for her help. Once they'd eaten, Charity told Isabella to take the forward bunk with her son and together they made up the two couches for her parents.

"I will consider it an honor and a pleasure if you would allow me to help you sail," the old man said. His eyes shown with a sparkle of life that wasn't there earlier.

"Rest with your wife," Charity said, smiling. "You can take the watch in two hours."

Once everyone was bedded down, Charity returned to the helm. *Wind Dancer* was living up to her name, dancing through the water once again, quartering the light easterly breeze, her sails close-hauled and making seven knots toward Key West.

Her inflatable Zodiac was plenty large enough to carry the four people and their meager belongings. The engine was a nearly new Johnson fifteen-horsepower two-stroke. It used about two gallons per hour at ten miles per hour. The trouble would be having enough gas to get there. Charity only had two gas tanks, each one holding five gallons. If seas were calm, the little dinghy could make it about fifty miles and arrive on Smathers Beach on reserves.

Charity plotted a new course, aiming the boat like an arrow toward Key West's tourist gathering spot, one of the few sand beaches in the Florida Keys. It was the nearest place the Zodiac could land safely.

Isabella climbed up through the hatch. "May I join you?" she whispered in heavily accented English.

Without waiting for an answer, she sat on the starboard bench, close to Charity. "You are not going to visit Mexico," Isabella said.

Charity just stared at her in the dim light emanating from the cabin. *Was that a challenge?* she thought.

"You are running," Isabella said. "How you say? Fleeing?"

The woman said it as though she was no stranger to the concept. *Not just fleeing Cuba, though,* Charity thought. She decided that she could trust this woman who had been through so much. At least a little.

Charity spoke in Spanish with a fluent Cuban inflection. "No, Isabella. I am an American citizen. My husband died two years ago. If anyone in America asks who helped you, this is what you must tell them."

Isabella was startled at the change in dialect. She thought for a moment, glancing at the sophisticated navigation equipment hidden in the old wheel pedestal.

"May I ask why you are going to Mexico?"

"Yes, but if anyone in America asks about me, what I just told you is all that you know. Do you understand?"

Isabella studied Charity's face a moment through dark brown eyes. She'd found one of Charity's hair ties, and her thick, wavy black hair was pulled back in a ponytail. Isabella's eyes sparkled in the moonlight, and she seemed to come to some conclusion.

"You are not running from something," Isabella said. "You are running after someone. A man." She didn't phrase it as a question, but a simple statement of fact.

Charity didn't reply, simply watched the woman watching her. Finally, Isabella whispered, "My mother once had the charm. She lost it to old age, but she passed it on to me. You will kill this man you seek and many others. I know this to be a good thing. One day, you will return to America, but not for some time. When you do arrive there, you will find me and Roberto, but Mama and Papa will have gone home to be with Jesus by then. However, they will die as free people in a free land. I will tell no one of these things, only that which you have told me to say."

Without another word, Isabella rose and went to the cabin, climbing down the ladder, without looking back. *Charm?* Charity thought. The Caribbean islands are full of tales of shamans and mystics, though she'd never met one. Charity knew there was nothing on board that pointed to her real identity, or her objective and mission. *Could this woman be the real thing?*

An hour later, while Charity was still puzzling over what Isabella had told her, the old man climbed quickly and silently up the ladder. He stood on the tilted deck and turned his face toward the wind, looking up at the sails and then out beyond the bow at the sea, his silver hair blowing back from his forehead.

He has to be in his sixties, at least, Charity thought. He still carried himself like a much younger man, though. Judging from the way he moved with the boat, it was obvious he was no stranger to the sea.

Finally, he turned around, and he was smiling. In very good English he said, "With your permission, *Capitán,* I will inspect the rigging for you."

Charity returned his smile and nodded. Alonzo turned and, without the aid of either the rail or the handholds along the side of the cabin, he walked forward, along the port side. With a touch from an experienced hand, he tested the standing rigging for tautness. Moments later, he returned on the starboard side to the cockpit and sat down beside Charity.

"Your *barca* is well and good," he reported. "And quite a beautiful vessel." The sparkle in his eyes and the smile on his face told Charity what he wanted most just now.

"Would you like to take the helm?" she asked, standing.

"I would like that very much," he replied and slid over behind the helm. He glanced down at the displays on the screens below the pedestal with its many switches. Then his eyes fell on the antique compass, mounted in its bezel on top of the pedestal. He glanced up at the stars that filled the night sky, his eyes brimming slightly. "We are on course for America."

Charity reached past his knee, found the switch for the autopilot and turned it off. "*Wind Dancer* is now under your full control, Alonzo."

The old man lovingly took the wheel in his twisted fingers. Charity noticed that they weren't so much contorted by arthritis, or years of pulling fishing nets. His fingers fit the wheel perfectly.

Glancing over at Charity, his smile broadened. "I am a sailor. But the government sent me to the fields, when I grew to be too old, to cut the sugarcane."

"Age does not make a man one thing or another," she said. "The salt water still courses through your veins. I can see that."

Alonzo looked up at the sails, the main luffing slightly. Charity scooted over closer and showed him the three switches that operated the sheet winches. "Foresail is the top one. The jib is below that, and the main below the jib. Try it."

Reaching down, Alonzo toggled the main sheet winch for a second, and the mainsail luffed even more. Toggling the switch the other way, he bent the boom inward a few inches until the snapping ceased.

"It is much easier than the winch handles," Alonzo said.

"You can easily single-hand the *Dancer* in a whole gale," Charity said.

Alonzo checked the compass and made a slight adjustment to the wheel. "Yes, I believe I could."

"When did you first take to the sea, Alonzo?"

"As a boy, not much older than Roberto. My father was a fisherman. He sailed a working sloop designed by the same man who designed this one. The name? It is very appropriate. She dances to a quick and happy tune."

"Thank you," Charity said. "I think so, as well."

"I worked for my father until I was old enough to buy my own boat. It was not as fine as his, and many leagues distant from this fine boat. But it was mine. However, I did not like the fishing so much."

"What did you do?"

Alonzo grinned. "Do you know that I am eighty-three years old? It is true. Rosina is my second wife. I buried my first wife of thirty years, long ago. We had two strapping sons. All lost to a hurricane, while I was at sea. Rosina is much younger than I. We have been married now for over thirty years. Isabella is my only child left, and Roberto my only heir."

He said this as if it was of great importance, though judging from the pitiful condition of their belongings, Roberto wouldn't be inheriting much.

"I once owned property," Alonzo said, continuing his story, as if reading Charity's mind. "A fine plantation house on a hill, overlooking Arroyos de Mantua, not far from the sea. The house is gone now, lost to the same tempest that took my first family. But the land is still there. When the bearded one is gone, my grandson can claim it as the rightful owner."

"It's worth a lot? This land?"

"Dirt is dirt," he said. Then, with a mischievous grin and a wink, he added, "But a man can put something under that dirt to make the land much more valuable."

"If you didn't fish when you were a young man, what did you do with this boat of yours?" Charity asked. She was enchanted with old Alonzo's melodious voice and his tales from long ago. She would never have guessed him to be in his eighties.

"I was born into America's Prohibition," Alonzo continued. "I've been to America many times since then. I was only six years old the first time I made the crossing with my father. We carried rum to Cayo Hueso. Many still called it that, back then.

"I learned something very valuable then. If something is illegal in America, it will be in high demand. As a young man with his own boat, I made the crossing many, many times. Twice a week, for many years. I carried people mostly, but deep in the bilge, I carried marijuana."

"You were a smuggler?" Charity asked, grinning with delight.

"A very good smuggler," he replied. "The son of a sail-or and smuggler. For many years, I rode on the wind that my forefathers, for several generations before me, had also harnessed. Everything I took to America, or brought back, I owned. I didn't transport freight for other people."

"Let me get this straight, Alonzo. You bought marijua-na in Cuba and smuggled it into the United States?"

"No," he replied. "I grew it myself and paid only pen-nies for the seed. I made enough money in ten years to last two lifetimes."

Charity couldn't help but laugh. Then a thought oc-curred to her. "You bought the plantation with your smuggling money?"

"Yes, I bought two hundred and forty acres. Very good tobacco land it was. With a fine plantation home and a number of curing barns for the tobacco. I became a *torce-doro*, a cigar roller. My sons and I made some of the fin-est cigars in the world. This was the time just before the bearded one. After the *revolución*, my land, as well as most every other man's land, was taken by the govern-ment. The people were forced to do this or that, whatev-er the government determined was best. I was sent back to the sea to fish. Did I tell you I didn't like the fishing so much?"

Charity laughed again. "Yes, Alonzo, you did. What happened to your tobacco plantation?"

"The government seized it. The fine home was turned into a business. The *torcedoros* working for us were forced to take a much lower wage and the cigars weren't as good as they once were. My family was allowed to con-tinue living there, as overseers, but the government said

I would fish. I was at sea when the storm took my home and family."

Alonzo looked out over the dark sea for a moment, as if remembering his first wife and their sons. "Now, they say I am too old to fish, or even to work the cane fields. So, the government cast me and Rosina aside and we could no longer afford the tiny house they put us in. Isabella worked in an office, her husband an officer in the navy. They lived much better than our little house, so they took us in. Roberto, the father, was killed just a year ago."

Alonzo let out a great sigh. "The government told Isabella she had to move to another house after that. And that she could not take me and Rosina with her. Her new house was not far from Guadiana Bay. It was there that I built our boat, while Rosina hid with friends in Playa Colorada. Two nights after I finished building it, we met you, Gabriela."

"Your daughter risked everything?" Charity asked in amazement. "She gave up her job? To protect you and her mother and risk everything to bring you to America."

"Sí," Alonzo replied, with a shrug. "It is what family does. It is not forever. The bearded one grows old. Faster than I do. He has grown fat on the people's *teta*. He is soft and will not last much longer. When he is gone, Isabella can bring Roberto back to his homeland to reclaim his birthright. He will know where to dig a hole and he will live a life of luxury, taking care of his mother, as she has done for me and my lovely Rosina." Then again, with the same mischievous grin and another wink he asked, "Did you know she is much younger than me?"

Charity laughed again. The laughing felt good. It was something she hadn't done much of in the last few years.

"Alonzo, you are a dog."

"*Sí, muchacha*, I am the dog. When Rosina is gone, I may charm *you* out of *your* pants."

Charity grinned at the old pervert and checked her watch. It was still three hours until daylight.

"Go, *Preciosa*. Get rested. I was sleeping for many hours before you wrecked my little *barca*. I will sail this fine boat on this course until you awaken."

Charity had no qualms about trusting her boat to the old man. He'd probably made this crossing more times than she'd gone grocery shopping.

"*Buenas noches*, Alonzo," Charity said, rising and patting the weathered hand on the wheel.

CHAPTER TWELVE:

S ix hours later, Charity awoke. The light streaming through the portholes on the starboard side told her it was already daylight. Sitting up quickly, she bumped her shoulder on the low underside of the side deck. Rising and rubbing her shoulder, she looked around the salon.

The quarter berth on the other side had been rearranged back to a couch. Glancing forward, Charity saw that the small vee-berth was made up and the cabin empty.

Charity climbed quickly up the ladder to the cockpit. Alonzo and his family were all sitting in the early-morning sun, little Roberto on his grandfather's lap, helping steer *Wind Dancer*.

"Good morning, *Preciosa*," Alonzo said. "It is such a fine morning for the sailing. You looked so peaceful in sleep, I did not wish to disturb you."

Sitting down on the other side of the helm, Charity glanced at the electronics. The small radar and chart plotter screens were turned off, as was the autopilot. She switched on the two screens and, according to the plotter, they'd traveled almost eighty miles and were no more than a quarter mile off the course she'd plotted the night before.

"My apologies," the old man said. "The light from the little televisions made it hard to see the stars. There was no show on them anyway."

"You sailed eighty miles, using only the compass?"

"I've sailed many thousands of miles," Alonzo replied. "All with nothing but the stars to guide my way. The compass only points to one of them, so I rarely use it. The stars are timeless and predictable. They tell me where I am and where I am going."

Smiling at the old man, Charity said, "I have a friend that says the same thing. You're a celestial navigator?"

"He was his father's navigator when he was just a boy," Rosina said, smiling.

"We are nearing America," Alonzo said. "It is perhaps five hours away."

Glancing at the plotter, Charity saw that he was very close. The ETA displayed four hours and forty-five minutes to Key West at current speed.

"The wind has picked up," Charity noted.

"Sí, and changed direction," Alonzo said. "A storm is brewing far to the north in the Gulf. We crossed the Stream an hour ago, at dawn. It was a special feeling for me."

We'll be within range of the Zodiac by early afternoon, Charity thought.

"You and your family will be in America before night-fall," Charity whispered to Alonzo. "You are an extraordinary sailor. May I bring you coffee, *Capitan*?"

The old man beamed. "*Sí, café!* For little Roberto, as well. He will become a great sailor, just like the men before him for six generations."

Going below, Charity switched on the coffeemaker, having already set it up the night before, while she and Isabella made soup and sandwiches.

Isabella came down the ladder, joining Charity. "You have given my father purpose again, Gabriela. I have never seen him like this in my whole life. Thank you."

"Your father is a unique man," Charity said. "In America, he will be called a Renaissance man." She stopped what she was doing and looked at Isabella. Though she was only a year or two older than Charity, the lines in her face made her appear much older. "Do you have relatives in America? Anyone that can help you get started?"

"Both of my father's brothers went to America long ago," Isabella said. "I have many cousins in Miami. Most are my mother's age, their children my age. We will be fine when we arrive. Father will take us to them and they will help us. It is what families do."

Charity poured coffee into a large thermos while considering the comment that both father and daughter had made. Her own family were all dead, and the only people close to her were those on her team, who she had left behind.

What coffee was left in the pot, she poured into two large mugs, only filling them halfway. Handing one to Isabella, she lifted her mug. "To your future in America."

Together, the two women sliced a loaf of Cuban bread that hadn't gotten wet in the raft and put bananas and mangoes into a small basket. They carried everything, along with three more mugs, up to the cockpit.

Wind Dancer sailed on through the morning. Alonzo kept her very close to the course on the plotter, though he never once looked down at it. Instead, he enthralled his shipmates with sea stories from long ago, while sailing by the compass.

By noon, *Wind Dancer* was within thirty miles of the Marquesas. They'd backtracked in just twelve hours what it'd taken Charity a day and a half to sail, running before the wind. They were now within the dinghy's range of Key West.

Charity rose and motioned to Isabella. "Will you help me get the dinghy ready, Isabella?"

"We are that close?" the woman asked.

"In the dinghy it will take four more hours. I must get back on my course to Mexico. Do not worry, the engine is new. You'll have no trouble getting there before dinnertime."

"Will you not need it?" Alonzo asked. The look on his face told Charity that he was hoping to sail right into Key West Bight.

"I'll get another, or return for it," Charity replied, thinking of her timetable. "I have to be in Mexico within five more days. This is as far as I can take you."

"It is alright, Father," Isabella said. "I know we will make it. Gabriela has an important engagement in Mexico."

Some of the sparkle left the old man's eyes, then quickly returned. "I will build my own boat in America, just like this one," he said, smiling.

After Alonzo furled the sails, it only took a few minutes to get the large rubber boat off its mount on the foredeck and into the water. Lifting the lid under the port bench, Charity removed the engine and stepped down into the dinghy to mount it.

The gas tanks were bulky, but Isabella managed to get them over the side, where Charity could set them up in the dinghy. Pumping the ball in the gas line, she explained to Alonzo how the little outboard operated. It started instantly, with only a slight tug on the starter cord.

Assured by the sound of the little engine, Alonzo and Rosina began to hand down their belongings. Charity shut off the outboard and stored the family's belongings along the sides of the inflatable, leaving room in the middle for Rosina and Roberto and a spot in the bow for Isabella. She would have to visually guide her father, as they neared Smathers Beach.

"Do you know the beach on the southeast side of Cayo Hueso?" Charity asked Alonzo.

"Very well," he said. "But I will go to the Mallory Docks."

"You'll never get close," Charity said. "Too many boats. Besides, things have changed there, and you won't like it."

"Why the beach?" Alonzo asked, puzzled.

"It's important that you get ashore as quickly as possible. Until your feet are on American soil, you can be returned to Cuba. Make for the beach, it is the best landing place. With Isabella watching for rocks, you can run right up onto the sand. When your feet are out of the water and you are standing on the beach, you will be Americans. Tell the first people you see on the beach, that you are Cuban refugees seeking asylum and ask them to call the authorities."

"Just like that?" Isabella asked.

"Yes," Charity replied. "In America, it is called 'feet dry.' Any Cuban national who gets ashore in America is granted immediate refugee status and permitted to stay. But your feet must be on dry land."

Placing the ladder over the gunwale, Alonzo helped his wife down into the Zodiac. Then Isabella climbed down, Roberto clinging to his mother's neck once more. She took Charity in her free arm, hugging her close in the pitching boat.

"Be careful, Gabriela," Isabella whispered. "I fear there is danger and pain ahead for you. But you will overcome both. The amount of pain will depend on how much you expose yourself to others."

"Take good care of your family, Isabella."

Climbing up to the cockpit, Charity turned and faced the old Cuban smuggler. "*Vaya con dios, Alonzo.*"

"Fair winds and a following sea, Gabriela," Alonzo said. "You have done so much for me and my family. I will dream of sailing this boat every night, and I will pray to San Cristóbal for your safe passage."

"Be careful," she warned. "If you have trouble, do you know the Marquesas?"

"Pretty fish to look at, but not many to catch," he replied with a knowing grin. "I have hidden there from the authorities many times."

"This doesn't surprise me," Charity said, smiling down at the white-haired man. "The Marquesas are part of America. Stop there before continuing to Key West. I put a camera in the emergency kit. Go ashore and find something permanent. There are a number of wrecks and abandoned boats along the shore. Have Isabella take a photograph of you on the beach, with one of these in the background. If you are stopped before reaching Key West, the picture will prove that you were on American soil before you were stopped."

The old man took Charity in his arms, hugging her tightly. Before releasing her, he kissed both her cheeks. "We will see one another again."

"I look forward to that day, Alonzo. Now go. Take your family to America, so Roberto can grow up a free man."

He stood on his toes and kissed her on the forehead, before scrambling quickly down the ladder. His new purpose in life seemed to renew his old body with vigor. The little engine started on the first pull, and Charity tossed the painter to Isabella. Within seconds, the little Zodiac was up on top of the waves, heading toward America.

CHAPTER THIRTEEN:

The wind continued to change direction throughout the afternoon. Within two hours of sending Alonzo and his family off to Key West, it was blowing at a steady twelve knots out of the south-southeast.

With the sails close-hauled, the apparent wind direction was out of the south at fifteen knots, and *Dancer's* speed was pushing nine. Charity calculated that she'd reach the spot where she'd collided with the Montoya family by midnight, having lost a day of travel time.

Feeling refreshed after they'd allowed her to sleep late, she was prepared for the coming night, with a new strategy. At sunset, she planned to sleep for one hour, then wake and be alert for half an hour. That would give her a full seven hours of sleep over the eleven hours between sunset and sunrise.

With the sun nearing the horizon again, Charity heard a pair of whooshing sounds, one after the other. Knowing what it was, she unclipped her safety line and attached it to the port cable rail, then went forward, checking the rigging and equipment. When she reached the bow, she waited a moment, looking ahead.

Suddenly a pair of dolphins rose to the surface, riding her bow wave for a second before separating and submerging. She knelt down and peered over the bow. The two dolphins were swimming effortlessly just below the surface, easily keeping pace with the fast-moving *Wind Dancer*. Surfers ride on top of a wave using gravity, but dolphins use the force of the displaced water below the surface and ride along on the pressure bulge.

The larger one surfaced, blowing air and spray right in Charity's face. She couldn't help herself and started laughing. Among sailors, having dolphins ride your bow wave was considered a good omen. She certainly hoped so.

When Charity returned to the cockpit, she went down to the galley and made a sandwich, using the last of the Montoyas' bread loaf. Before returning to the helm, she checked her laptop for messages and found none. Taking her sweater, a pillow, and a blanket, she returned to the helm to watch the sunset.

As the sun began to slip below the horizon, *Wind Dancer* was three hundred and fifty miles from Progresso and over seven hundred miles from Alvarado. If the wind continued to blow out of the southern quadrant and she could average seven knots, she could still clear customs and take a short rest in the Yucatan port city, before arriving in Alvarado in less than five days.

CHAPTER
FOURTEEN:

After eight days of training with the small automatic weapons, Hussein was satisfied, even if Karim didn't agree. But he'd allowed Karim to work for another three days with three of the men who weren't as adept at shooting.

In Hussein's tent, Awad and Karim sat on the bare ground, waiting for the leader to finish his opium pipe. Finally, the blue-gray smoke curled from his mouth and up to the vents in the tent roof.

"The American celebration is in nine days," Hussein said. "It will take us two days to reach the city of San Antonio. Between now and then, you two will work with the others. Teach them enough about American ways so they will not be so noticeable."

"What ways in particular?" Karim asked.

"Foremost, once we leave here, there will be no more prayer. I watched the Americans at their base in Cuba. They have a way about them. The way they move and walk, like they are invincible. When you and Awad first arrived here, you moved like them. The men must learn to mimic this."

"We will do all we can," Awad replied, not exactly sure what the leader was talking about.

"I have arranged a truck that will carry all of us to Reynosa, on the border. This leg of the journey is one thousand kilometers. From there, it is another five hundred kilometers to San Antonio."

"How long will it take?" Karim asked.

"We will leave the camp two hours before the sun sets, six days from now. The truck will pick us up on the road to the west when it is dark, and we will arrive in Reynosa before noon, four days from now. There, we will rest until nightfall, then split into three groups and make the trip across the border at night, rejoining in San Antonio. Each of us will lead one of these groups, to minimize the chance of being seen."

"How are we to get from the border to San Antonio?" Awad asked.

Hussein extended his arm behind him and pulled a small brown satchel from under his cot. Reaching in, he withdrew two small packages and handed one to each man.

"Inside, you will find maps and five thousand American dollars, plus fake credit cards for each of you. We will hire someone to smuggle our group across the border separately, using the money. They call these smugglers *coyotes*. Each group will go to a different American town near the border. There, each group will rent a car or van to drive the last leg to San Antonio. Be careful to drive exactly the speed limit, so as not to be stopped by the infidel's police."

"Slightly over the speed limit," Karim advised. "Nobody in America obeys the speed laws. Doing so will attract attention."

"They disregard their own laws as well as the law of Allah?" Hussein asked, rhetorically. "Very well, Karim. That is why you and Awad are with us. You know the ways of the infidels."

"The truck you hired?" Awad asked. "Can the driver be trusted?"

"No, he cannot. The truck was hired through the Reynosa drug cartel. These people are ruthless and will do anything for money. Do not discuss our destination or anything else with the driver, nor with the coyotes that will smuggle you across."

"You have planned this well, Hussein," Karim said. "Where will we meet in San Antonio?"

"There is a hotel, not far from the place called River Walk, a short walk to where the tour boats pick people up. It is called Wyndham. At the hotel, each group will split up into groups of two each and check into three rooms at the hotel. You should do this at different times, not all together. The three of us will have separate rooms. Each of you will arrange this with the men in your group."

Awad and Karim both nodded. "It is a good plan," Karim agreed.

As Hussein packed his hookah with more opium, he waved his hand toward the tent flap. "Go now. Get rested. Tomorrow we will start learning the infidel's ways. In four days, just before we leave, we will practice with the weapons again, for two days. On the sixth day, we will each spend the day alone in prayer."

Outside, Karim offered Awad a cigarette, lighting both with a single match. The two men walked to the far side of the camp, away from the other tents. Most of the men had gone to sleep or were preparing to do so. Only a single sentry in the middle of the half circle of tents noticed them.

"Is it a good plan?" Awad asked in a quiet voice.

Karim considered the question for a moment. "Yes, I think it is," he responded. "If Hussein will stick to it. You know as well as I do about his history of rash decisions."

"But he always succeeded."

"All but the one time, when he was captured," Karim said. "Have you not heard what happened that day?"

"No, I have not."

"He and his fighters attacked a small village, not far from one of the American camps. They killed indiscriminately and rounded up all of the young women of the village. During the orgy of blood and carnal delight, the Americans slipped into the village, killing most of his fighters and taking the others prisoner, along with Hussein."

"You would have done differently?" Awad asked, taking a drag on the cigarette.

Karim looked down at the ground a moment. In the dappled light of the moon filtering through the trees, Awad saw the same sadistic grin their leader had displayed. "Yes," Karim said quietly. "I would have put the women to the blade and left the village before the Americans arrived."

Karim turned and walked off toward his tent, leaving Awad to his own thoughts. In truth, Awad had been swayed by the American lifestyle. He enjoyed the things that both Karim and Hussein detested. He especially enjoyed the American women, and those from his own country who had grown up in America.

Tired, Awad went to his own tent. As he was lying on his cot, he heard the rumble of distant thunder again. For just a moment, he thought it a bad omen.

CHAPTER FIFTEEN:

U sing her fake passport, Charity cleared Mexican customs in Progresso in the early afternoon. Sailing straight through the night for three consecutive nights, taking short naps between watches, had taken its toll. She spent the rest of the afternoon restocking *Wind Dancer* with food, water, and fuel. The fuel was expensive, but she needed very little. She wanted nothing more than a hot shower and get to bed shortly after sunset.

Shopping in the farmer's market near the marina, Charity negotiated with the men and women at the booths, buying plenty of fruits and vegetables at very good prices. At the few stalls that offered meat, it was priced very high. The chicken and pork she saw didn't appear as fresh as it ought to be. And nobody had beef that looked even remotely edible.

Returning to the marina, Charity encountered a fisherman who had just tied up and was unloading his catch.

Pointing to three large hogfish, obviously speared, she asked, "You are a scuba diver?"

The young Mexican man looked up. "Diver, yes. Scuba, no. It is not sporting to rely on tanks and equipment. I am Juan Ignacio."

On closer inspection, the fisherman appeared a few years older than Charity, maybe in his early thirties. Taller than most Mexican men, he wore only the lower half of a wetsuit, cut off below the knees. She thought him quite handsome.

"I am Gabriela Oritz," Charity said, sticking to the maiden name of her alias. "How much for the *viejas*?"

Juan smiled at her, displaying a row of perfect teeth, below a thin mustache. "For you, *señorita*? Thirty pesos each."

Charity smiled. Thirty pesos was less than two dollars and quite a deal. However, it was the custom to haggle over the price of anything. Placing her canvas bags full of produce on the dock, she knelt down and picked up the smallest, testing its weight.

Wiping her hand on a rag the man offered, she stood up, cocking her hip to the side, as she pretended to be considering the price. The pose had the desired effect. Juan stood up straighter and smiled up at her.

"I will give you sixty pesos for all three," Charity said, smiling back.

Juan's smile broadened. "Sixty pesos and a dance at the cantina this evening?" he asked, pointing to a small restaurant and bar just down the street.

She was planning to go to bed early, to take advantage of the receding tide just before sunrise. But, after three days of sailing, seeing nothing but an occasional oil

tanker, having a cold beer and a dance with a good-look-
ing man didn't seem like a bad idea. It'd been years since
she'd danced with anyone and quite a while since she'd
even been on a date.

"Sixty pesos and one dance," Charity replied. "I leave
with the morning tide." If possible, Juan's perfect smile
grew even wider. "And you buy me a beer," she added
with a smile.

"For that, Señorita, I will even clean them for you,"
Juan said. "Where is your boat?"

"You have a deal, Juan Ignacio," Charity said. "Let me
take my produce and put it away and I will be right back."

Without waiting for a reply, she picked up her bags
and sauntered down the dock toward *Wind Dancer*, tied
at the far end. Knowing that he was watching, she put a
bit more sway in her hips as she walked.

Fifteen minutes later, she returned. Juan was sitting
on a small stool. He'd finished unloading his catch into
a small two-wheeled cart, and covered it with ice. He'd
changed into jeans and a clean white T-shirt, wearing a
worn Tommy Bahama hat against the tropical sun.

As Charity approached, Juan stood quickly. Charity
immediately noticed that he was taller than she'd first
thought, nearly six feet. Removing his hat, he became
flustered. "My apologies, Señorita. I did not mean to be
so forward."

Charity found his sudden shy and chivalrous attitude
refreshing. "I have been in the United States for a few
years, Juan. You are quite the gentleman. I am looking
forward to dancing with a gentleman. Sunset at the cantina?"

Grinning, Juan picked up the six fillets from the top of the pile in his cart. "The light of the setting sun can only make a woman such as yourself even more beautiful, Señorita Gabriela."

Each fillet was carefully wrapped in brown wax paper, secured with a piece of twine. Charity stepped closer, opening her canvas bag. He put the fish in it and she reached into her pocket. Handing him sixty pesos, her fingers lingered on his palm for a second.

"Perhaps two dances," she said with a smile. Once more, she turned without another word and strolled back to her boat.

In the galley, she placed two of the packages in the tiny refrigerator and the rest in the freezer. She wanted to cook one before going to the cantina. With the *Dancer* connected to both shore power and freshwater, she'd been looking forward to a hot freshwater shower since arriving.

Opening her hanging closet, she realized that she didn't have a lot to choose from. Most of her clothes were rugged sailing attire, or black pants and shirts for her mission ahead. Of the two casual outfits in the closet, she chose a simple, dark blue dress made from lightweight material and laid it on the bunk.

With only the hot water turned on, Charity took a long shower, scrubbing her skin nearly raw with the brush. Turning the hot water off, she turned on the cold, gasping and flinching involuntarily, as it hit her skin. She rinsed for several minutes under the cold water, which reinvigorated her.

Wearing only panties and a white tank top, Charity went into the galley to prepare dinner. A friend back in Marathon, an old Jamaican chef, had given her several small containers, each holding an assortment of pre-mixed herbs and spices. Each container was labeled in simple handwriting with what it was to be used for. She opened the small cupboard and picked the container labeled "Swimmers."

While the fish sizzled in the skillet, Charity powered up her laptop to check for messages. Connecting to the email server, she saw there was a saved document in the draft file and clicked on it.

Latest satellite flyover shows no training activity in the crater. However, the noon and evening meals were prepared over the same fire as previous days.

Deleting the message, she wrote a short reply: *ETA Alvarado: 48 hours.* Saving the message, she rose and flipped the fish over in the skillet, then went forward to the vee-berth and quickly dressed.

After eating a light meal of fish and a small salad, Charity washed the dishes, leaving everything on the drainboard. Through the porthole, she could see the sun nearing the tops of the little houses that dotted the hillside on the other side of the small bay.

Going back to the forward berth, she pulled the bifold door closed. She checked herself in the narrow full-length mirrors mounted on the doors, and her black hair startled her. She had only seen herself with black hair several days earlier when she dyed it. Leaning closer, she inspected the roots. She'd need a touchup before long.

Stepping back, she smoothed the light fabric against her belly and turned, looking over her shoulder. The back of the dress was cut low, with thin spaghetti straps, accentuating her long, slim torso. Slipping her feet into a pair of leather thong sandals, she went aft to the ladder.

Closing the hatch securely, Charity knelt and opened the control panel. A touch of the lock button sent the heavy bolts into place and armed the security system. A tiny red LED light below the trim of the cabin roof began flashing. The light was the only warning an intruder would receive. If anyone attempted to force the hatch open, a very loud siren would begin wailing inside the cabin. She hoped the warning light would deter any would-be thieves.

Before exiting the cockpit, Charity looked all around the dock area before setting one last precaution. She didn't see anyone anywhere. A thin strand of monofilament fishing line, nearly invisible, hung from the forward rail at the gangplank. The end of it was tied in a loose loop, which she placed over a tiny nail on the inside of the aft rail post. Anyone coming aboard would knock it loose, but it was secured so lightly and was so thin, it wouldn't be felt as anything more than a strand of a spider's web.

Satisfied, Charity stepped over the line and made her way down the nearly empty dock. All of the fishermen had left their boats and gone home, but music emanated from a couple of cruising sailboats.

There was little traffic on the road as Charity jogged diagonally across, seeing Juan waiting on a stool, just outside the cantina. He rose quickly as she approached. Charity was pleased to see that he'd not bothered to shave the stubble on his face. He was dressed in black jeans and a Western-style shirt with pearl snaps instead of buttons, the top two undone.

"I was wrong," Juan said, his voice faltering slightly.

"Wrong about what?" Charity asked innocently.

"The setting sun does not make you more beautiful," he replied. "You make the sunset look simple and plain. Have you eaten?"

"Yes, blackened *vieja Mexicana*. It was delicious," she replied as Juan pulled the door open for her.

The interior of the cantina was simply decorated. A long bar took up more than half of the far wall with a dozen or more stools. Two were occupied by a couple of fishermen who apparently hadn't gotten any further from their boats than the door of the cantina. To the right were a number of tables, all empty but one. A young Mexican couple was dining by the window, sitting very close together and oblivious to anyone or anything around them. To the left was a small dance floor and an even smaller stage, where a band was just setting up their equipment.

At a corner table, Juan held a chair for Charity. When he sat down, the bartender approached, carrying menus. "May I get you something to drink?" he asked.

"Two Montejos," Juan replied. The bartender left the menus and went back to the bar, just as the band started warming up.

"This is a good band," Juan said, making small talk.

Charity looked toward the stage. A tall, thin man was tuning an upright bass, as two more men plucked at acoustic Mexican guitars, all plugged into small amplifiers and speakers. A girl of about fifteen or sixteen was dwarfed behind a drum set at the back of the stage, a microphone dangling precariously from a makeshift stand in front of her. Another microphone stand was at the front of the stage, next to it a stool with a trumpet resting on it. Without introduction, the young girl tapped a measure on the edge of one of her drums, and the musicians began a mariachi tune. The singer was nowhere to be seen.

The bartender brought their beers, dripping cold, and placed them on the table. Juan gathered up the menus and handed them to the man. "We have already eaten, Manuel," he said.

Turning to Charity, he said, "I have lived here all my life, so I know you are not from this area."

"I am from Mexico City," Charity lied. "But, as I said, I have been living in the United States for the last few years."

They talked for a few minutes, while the band continued the fast-tempo tune. Charity told him about her make-believe life in the US, and he told her about free diving for the fish he sold. As if the music had drawn them in, a nearly steady stream of people began to fill the cantina. Mostly men sat at the bar, but a few couples soon filled the surrounding tables, and a couple of apparently unattached women sat together at the bar.

Not a lot different than the meat markets back home, Charity thought.

The band finished their tune as a beautiful raven-haired woman stepped out of a door next to the stage. Her hair was thick, flowing down across her shoulders. She wore a snug white tank top and tight black jeans. Everyone in the cantina began cheering, Juan the most enthusiastic of them all.

As the band began a slow, sexy melody, Juan turned to Charity and said, "The singer and drummer are my sisters, Rosa and Carmen."

Juan was right, the band was very good. Rosa, the singer, had a sultry voice, and sang about a lost lover as if she were talking to every man in the cantina. When the song ended, several men at the bar stood up, applauding.

Rosa bowed and then waved to Juan. Taking the microphone in one hand and leaning it toward Charity, she said, "I think my brother might like to play for you. Can you encourage him?"

There was more applause and cheers. "Would you mind?" Juan asked Charity. "Only one song, though."

Charity nodded enthusiastically, and Juan stood up, striding confidently toward the stage, where he picked up the trumpet and fingered the valves several times. He leaned over to the girl behind the drums and whispered something to her and Rosa. Then, bringing the horn to his lips, Carmen measured a beat on a cymbal.

Charity was surprised when he began to play a fast-paced bluesy kind of tune, not the typical Mexican-style melody. Only Carmen and the bass player joined in, while the two guitarists went to the bar and ordered a beer.

Behind a speaker, Rosa retrieved a saxophone. She and Juan began playing off one another, obviously very accustomed to each other's style. The tune they played was hypnotic, building to several crescendos.

When they finished, Juan returned to the table amid a long round of applause. "I really wasn't expecting that," Charity said as the bartender brought them two more bottles of beer and the band broke into a salsa tune, with Rosa on the sax.

Several couples made their way to the dance floor, and Juan leaned toward Charity. "Do you know the salsa?"

"It has been a while," Charity replied. Juan stood and extended his hand. Charity took it and he led her to the dance floor.

The band melded from one salsa number into another for ten straight minutes, as the dancers spun and gyrated to the sultry beat. Charity was thoroughly enjoying herself, allowing Juan to spin her around and march her backward, his hand low on her swaying hips.

When they finally returned to the table, they were both sweating from the exertion. They had one more beer before Charity said, "I really do have to leave early, Juan. The outgoing tide is two hours before sunrise."

"Will you allow me to walk you back? The streets of Progresso can be dangerous at night."

"Yes," Charity said, though she really didn't feel unsafe walking at night in a strange city. "I'd like that."

Together, they left the cantina, the music fading into the background as they walked toward the marina.

"Where will you go in the morning?" Juan asked, shuffling along with his hands in his pockets.

Charity appreciated that he'd not asked if she was traveling alone and took his arm. Most men scoffed at the idea that a woman could sail across the ocean solo.

"Laguna de Tampamachoco," Charity replied. "My family has a small home with a dock on the bay. Then I will drive from there to our home in Mexico City."

Approaching an alley, Charity saw a man leaning against the wall of a shop near the opposite curb, one leg up, the sole of his boot planted against the wall. He wore a cowboy hat pulled down and his face was lowered, so Charity couldn't see it.

As Charity and Juan stepped off the curb, the man pushed away from the wall, seeming to turn down the alley. When they reached the halfway point in the alley, the man turned and was suddenly standing right in front of Juan. He held a long stiletto-type knife low against his right thigh.

"Do not cry out," the man said to Juan. "Or I will kill the woman. Give me your money."

Assuming that the tall, broad-shouldered man was the greater threat was a serious mistake on the robber's part. In the time it took him to make his demand of Juan, Charity had imperceptibly stepped out of her sandals.

Juan started to say something, and the robber raised the knife menacingly. Charity's right hand flew up, grasping the man's knife hand by the wrist and forcing it higher. At the same time, she stepped past him with her left leg, taking the man off balance. Bringing her right knee up into his groin, she powered him back with enough force to lift him off the ground.

Charity followed the man as he went backward, his knife hand still high and of no use to him. The man started to double over in pain, and Charity jerked his arm downward, stepping past him and spinning to her right, still holding his wrist. The man's forward momentum as he was doubling over, coupled with Charity's spin, sent him flying around her. Continuing forward, she whipped the man's body past her on the other side of a lamppost.

The robber's body weight, which propelled him forward on one side of the post, and Charity's continued forward movement on the other side both came to a quick stop, as his forearm impacted the steel post with a sickening crack. Both bones in his forearm snapped, piercing the skin and tearing through his shirtsleeve as blood poured from the wound.

Screaming in pain, the man dropped the knife and held his shattered wrist in his hand as he staggered and leaned heavily against the wall.

But Charity didn't stop there. Using the lamppost for leverage, she flung herself around it in a reverse spin, kicking high with her outside leg. The bottom of her foot connected with the back of the man's neck with a popping sound, just as her other foot came off the ground.

The man's scream ended abruptly as his inert body lunged forward from the impact. His face hit the gravel surface of the alley with a thud. Charity landed lightly, crouched on bare feet astride him with her right hand cocked back, ready to punch if he moved.

He didn't move.

Juan took a step toward her, and Charity's head whipped around, slinging her hair back over her shoulder. Her right leg came over the man's body and she crouched low in a fighter's stance, the body between her and the possible new threat.

Juan stopped in his tracks, the ferocious look on Charity's face freezing him in place. Slowly he raised his hands. "I would ask if you are alright," he said. "But that would be a stupid question." Glancing down at the man on the ground, he asked, "Is he dead?"

Charity stepped over the robber and grabbed Juan's hand, moving him quickly down the sidewalk. "If he's not," she said, "he will be soon. Come, we have to get away from here."

At first, she nearly had to drag Juan across the street toward the marina. Once he sensed her urgency, he quickly trotted along with her. "My boat," he said. "We can watch from the cabin."

Together, they hurried along the dock and stepped down into his fishing boat. Crossing the small cockpit and moving up the port-side deck, they entered the wheelhouse, both out of breath.

"I think you killed that man," Juan said, lifting one of the blinds that covered the window and peering out. "I don't think anyone saw what happened, though."

"Probably," Charity said. "That kind of life? It was bound to happen sooner or later." She was suddenly filled with an urgency she hadn't felt in over two years. Looking past Juan, she saw an open door, a neat tiny cabin beyond it, with a desk and a small bunk.

Juan wheeled and looked at her. Charity stood in the center of the wheelhouse, feet apart, hands on her hips. The soft light of the moon filtering through the blinds played diagonal stripes across her body as her breasts rose and fell, breathing heavily.

Charity's hair was disheveled from the scuffle. Her skin glistened with light beads of sweat, and her dress clung to her body, outlining her form.

Charity took a slow step toward Juan, then another. Suddenly she leaped at him, wrapping her arms around his neck and one leg around his thigh. Driving him back against the wall, she found his mouth with hers.

Breaking free for a moment, Charity ripped the snaps loose on his shirt and pressed her body hard against him, only the thin fabric of her dress separating the two.

Grinding her body against him, she gripped the hair on the back of his head and kissed him passionately, feeling nothing but animal lust and physical need.

CHAPTER SIXTEEN:

Five days after McDermitt was rescued, Director Stockwell's plan was falling somewhat into place. Everyone who knew Charity Styles assumed she would have stability issues. After what she'd been through, some instability was to be expected. Stockwell didn't particularly like this part of the plan, but it was necessary.

However, Stockwell knew full well just how stable the woman was. He'd spoken at length with the doctors who had treated her. They'd explained how the woman had compartmentalized her negative feelings toward those who had tortured her. The doctors had told him that compartmentalization was a psychological defense mechanism used to avoid the mental discomfort they called cognitive dissonance, where a person might have conflicting values or emotions within themselves.

Charity Styles was one of the few people who could completely compartmentalize things at will. She could function for months, even years—maybe for the rest of her life—as a perfectly stable person, never opening that part of her subconscious. But, if need be, she could open it and use all the hate and anger stored there. Afterward, the doctors agreed, she could close the compartment to her conscious mind off again and return to having full control of herself.

Stockwell had seen firsthand what happened when she opened up that part of her mind. He'd attended a number of martial arts events she'd competed in, fighting against some of the top hand-to-hand fighters in the world. He'd also spoken at length with McDermitt, regarding the death of Jason Smith. Smith had been the director before Stockwell but had gone rogue after his posting to Djibouti, hiring mercenaries to kill McDermitt and Commander Livingston. They'd also learned that Smith had arranged his own wife's death years earlier in order to inherit her fortune. If that wasn't enough, he'd been responsible for the death of a young Marine that Styles had become close to.

McDermitt had located Smith and, though the former CIA man had held a gun on McDermitt, Styles had stepped in and killed him with her bare hands. After it was over, McDermitt said she'd returned to her normally stable attitude. On the return trip to Florida, Styles had opened up twice to McDermitt, sharing things with him that she said she'd never told anyone, except the young Marine who Smith had killed.

Stockwell's plan was simple. Once the excitement of the rescue mission died down, it would be discovered that, in the heat of the mission, Styles had simply vanished, taking a half-million-dollar aircraft with her.

Stockwell had already set his fake retirement plan into motion and had spoken with the Homeland secretary about appointing McDermitt as the new director. His position would be a figurehead, someone in DC that all the members of the team knew and trusted, particularly Lieutenant Commander Deuce Livingston.

But McDermitt had turned the offer down cold. He had absolutely no interest in politics, city life, or advancement. The man was content to live out his life in seclusion, fishing, diving, and drinking.

McDermitt had even gone so far as to warn Livingston against taking the position as Stockwell's second choice. Based on ability alone, Livingston was the better decision. But his leadership of the team of operators in Homestead was more vital.

In the end, Livingston had accepted the promotion to commander and the appointment as acting director, and it had been announced that Stockwell was retiring from public life.

Styles had disappeared without a trace. A bogus FBI investigation had been started and quickly filed as a cold case, with no leads and no witnesses. The Coast Guard had been dispatched, searching all of Florida Bay and the Everglades for her downed aircraft. Nothing had been found. It had only taken one day before rumors started that she'd come unhinged during the rescue operation and stolen the aircraft, disappearing with a small fortune, her share of a treasure find orchestrated by McDermitt.

Stockwell had accepted an offer from McDermitt to work part-time on his charter boat, giving him a perfect cover. McDermitt only took one or two charters out a week, at best.

Now, just five days after McDermitt had been reunited with his daughter and friends, nearly everyone believed the ruse, though few spoke openly about it. Livingston and his wife had arrived in DC this morning and begun unpacking at their new home in Quantico.

In just a few minutes, the secretary would meet with both Stockwell and Livingston, transferring the office to the younger man. Before the sun went down, Stockwell would be on a G5, heading for the Florida Keys, appearing to begin a new life as a retired public servant.

The proximity and light duties of his cover job would allow Stockwell to move around the Caribbean Basin during his off days, helping Styles where he could and directing her where he couldn't.

Her first target had been chosen weeks before. A known terrorist detainee, more of a low-level thug, had been released from Guantanamo just over three years ago. He had been transferred to Uruguayan custody, but eight months later, he'd disappeared.

Hussein Seif al Din Asfour had reappeared on the battlefield in Afghanistan a year later, leading a group of fighters hiding out in the Arma Mountains.

Less than six months ago, a sharp-eyed analyst with the CIA had picked him up on a routine monitoring of worldwide airport security cameras. Unfortunately, the terrorist had disappeared before anyone could move against him.

Chatter among known terrorist groups put al Din Asfour as the leader of a cell located in the jungles of Guatemala. More information, gleaned from many sources, had al Din Asfour moving across the border into Mexico, and the cell disappearing in Guatemala.

It had been decided two weeks ago, by the Homeland secretary, that al Din Asfour had to be removed from the playing field once and for all. He would be Charity Styles's first test.

At present, Styles was on her way to Mexico, traveling slowly but steadily by sailboat toward the hiding place the terrorist cell had chosen on the peak of a dormant volcano in the Mexican state of Veracruz. Her last communication had her only two days from arriving in Alvarado and perhaps four days from finding and killing the terrorist.

Chatter on various terrorist websites pointed toward a possible attack against a soft target somewhere in South Texas on Armed Forces Day, which was in six days. It was believed that the cell on the San Martin Tuxtla volcano was training for this attack.

Not a lot of wiggle room, Stockwell thought.

Should Styles fail, the terrorist cell could be apprehended once they crossed the border. But detaining more terrorists in Guantanamo wasn't sitting well with several liberal presidential candidates, and an election was just a year and a half away. Some were even speaking openly of closing the detention camp there.

No, simply apprehending these terrorists in the United States wasn't something the secretary, nor the current president, wanted. If all went well, the terrorist leader would die in Mexico. Possibly a few of the other members of the cell as well.

"The secretary will see you now, Director," the aide said, bringing Stockwell back to the present.

Together, Stockwell and Livingston were shown into Secretary Chertoff's inner office.

"Congratulations on your promotion, Commander," the secretary said, rising from his chair and coming around the desk to shake Deuce's hand.

"Thank you, sir."

"Please have a seat," Chertoff said, motioning toward the two heavy leather chairs in front of the desk.

Once his guests were seated, the secretary leaned against his desk. "The president has approved your appointment as the acting Associate Director for Caribbean Counterterrorism, replacing Colonel Stockwell. It will, of course, have to be approved by Congress."

"I'm honored to even be considered, sir," Deuce said.

Stockwell turned to Deuce and said, "I asked the secretary to bring you up to speed personally on the situation with Charity Styles, Deuce. I'm afraid you're not going to like it."

Deuce looked from one to the other, obviously confused. He didn't believe the rumors about Charity stealing the chopper. If anything, he thought the helo must have had some kind of mechanical failure and gone down.

Finally, Secretary Chertoff went behind his desk, unlocked a drawer and withdrew a file with a top-secret cover sheet, marked Operation: Sea Fury. Handing the file to Deuce, the secretary explained to him the full scope of the operation. Stockwell was right—Deuce didn't like it at all.

"How many know about this, Mister Secretary?" Deuce asked, keeping his obvious agitation in check.

"Outside of this room, only one other person. The president."

"So, I'm expected to lie?"

"It has to be this way, son," the secretary replied. "Colonel Stockwell assured me that you're the kind of man who can put the mission before his own personal honor."

Deuce thought it over a minute. "Eventually, sir, the word will get out about what really happened. She'll be spotted in the vicinity of an assassination, or arrested entering a country with a phony passport, and someone will put two and two together."

"We've already taken steps to minimize that, if and when it happens," Stockwell said. "I agree. It's likely to happen. Hopefully, the revelation can be contained to only those in the intelligence and spec-ops communities. That's who will likely be the first to discover it."

Deuce stood and walked to the window overlooking Washington Navy Yard and the Anacostia River beyond it. He stared out toward the famous buildings and landmarks across the river. In the distance, he could just see the top of the Washington Monument.

Finally, he turned and faced the secretary and soon-to-be-former director. "I'll do what needs to be done, sir."

CHAPTER SEVENTEEN:

By the light of a high waning moon, *Wind Dancer* slowly motored through the inlet and into the Gulf of Mexico. Charity buried the memory of the night before and concentrated on the task at hand.

Clearing the jetty, she held a northern course, until she was a mile offshore. Then, turning west, she toggled all three switches, unfurling the sails. They snapped and filled in the light, but favorable, southerly breeze coming off the coast.

Wind Dancer heeled to starboard, accelerating, and Charity shut off the little diesel engine. Alvarado lay four hundred and thirty miles to the southwest. With luck, two days of sailing, arriving at dusk. But that would mean an average speed of seven knots.

She knew that she'd lose most of the south wind by the time she made it halfway. The storm in the Gulf had moved inland, way up into the Florida panhandle, and the wind would return to its typical pattern. She would once more have to run before the wind, blowing toward the warmer land mass of mainland Mexico. In this part of the Gulf, the typical winds blew a little more northerly, at least. For the next hundred miles, she'd have to get every knot of speed *Dancer* could muster.

Less than an hour later and fifteen miles out of Progresso, Charity engaged the autopilot. The computer turned the boat toward the southwest, trimming the sails for maximum efficiency. She'd let the computer do most of the sailing from here on, having learned to trust the system more.

The sun was just beginning to tinge the sky behind *Wind Dancer* as Charity went below to get something to eat and check the laptop for messages. She was still wearing the dress from the night before, having been too exhausted to change when she'd returned to *Wind Dancer*. She quickly went forward and changed into proper sailing attire, long pants and a long-sleeved shirt.

When she returned to the helm thirty minutes later, the sun was above the horizon behind her. A quick check of the helm told her that *Dancer* was sailing a steady eight knots. She ate sliced fruit and thought about the message she'd received.

It'd been five days since she'd veered away from the go-fast boat in Florida Bay. McDermitt and the rest of the team had returned to their lives and duties, nobody hurt. But Jesse had turned down the job offer to be Stockwell's successor. The director had seemed to think the man would accept it, but Charity had known all along that he wouldn't. Jesse had served as a Marine for twenty years, costing him two failed marriages. For the last two years, he'd been involved with Homeland Security and lost his wife to domestic terrorists. He'd already given far more than his fair share.

Instead, Commander Livingston had assumed the role, moving to DC within a few days of Charity's disappearance. The message had been from Deuce himself, reporting to her everything that had transpired and saying that even though he didn't like how it had happened, he'd help her in any way he could. At the end of the message, he'd wished her well and said that he and his wife would pray for her safe return.

As the morning bore on, Charity contemplated the last part of the message. She'd never known her boss to be a religious man. She did recall his saying once that there were no atheists on the battlefield. Aside from that one reference, she couldn't remember him mentioning religion or saying that he and his wife attended church.

Hours later, with little else to occupy her time, she went below and began putting together the equipment she'd need to take with her once she reached Alvarado. The original plan was to anchor in a secluded cove and use the Zodiac to transport things to a waiting car, once she'd secured one.

Now, she would be forced to tie up at a dock. Which would mean finding a marina where she could bring a car close to the boat. A person walking a long pier, dressed in black, and carrying a sniper rifle and gear, wouldn't go unnoticed, even in the middle of the night.

With luck, she'd arrive in Alvarado early enough in the evening to rent a car or truck for the fifty-mile drive to the southern slope of the volcano. Barring that, she'd have to wait and rent the car the next day. If she could then get her gear to it without drawing attention, she could drive to within a few miles of the volcano and wait for darkness. The tone of Deuce's message indicated that time was of the essence. He'd mentioned reports that an attack in South Texas was planned for Armed Forces Day, less than six days away. If it was this cell, they'd wait until the last minute to cross the border, which meant they'd leave the volcano in four days.

Best case, she'd have two nights in which to scout the enemy camp before taking her shot when the terrorists met for breakfast in the crater. Worst case would mean climbing to the high northern slope during the night and taking the shot the next morning.

As the afternoon turned into evening, Charity prepared for another night of sleeping at the helm in short naps.

CHAPTER EIGHTEEN:

Awad woke early. It was still dark when he rolled out his prayer mat for the morning prayer. When he finished, he rolled and stored his mat, picked up his backpack with the lightweight machine pistol inside and left the tent.

Fareed was on watch and had to be relieved so he could prepare the morning meal. Walking along the now-familiar path to the summit, Awad thought about the coming days. Today they were weapons training again, after a couple of days of him and Karim trying to teach the men a few words and phrases of English, and to act a little more like the infidels they hated so much. It was a lesson in futility.

Tomorrow was more weapons training, and after that, each man was to spend a full day in prayer, fasting after the morning meal. At least being on lookout, he wouldn't have to be shooting.

It took Awad twenty minutes to cross the crater, where they practiced shooting at a large round rock in the center, and climb up to the high spot where Fareed watched over the surrounding area. The only light to guide his way was the waning moon, now high overhead. In a few more days, they wouldn't even have that. Not that it mattered. They'd be gone.

"*As-salamu alaykum*," Fareed said as Awad stepped up onto the giant boulder that would be his perch for the next three hours. Since Fareed cooked all the meals, Awad was relieving him early, so he could get his cook fire started.

"*Wa-Alaikum-Salaam*," Awad replied. "You will remember to bring me something to eat, once the others have finished?"

The cook grinned. "I feel Faud may be right. You do have a tapeworm inside you. Yes, I will make sure to bring you plenty."

"Have you seen or heard anything?"

"A few sounds down in the darkness below, animals, probably. I have not seen any vehicles on the road all night."

"Not even on the main road to the west?"

"No, nothing at all," Fareed replied, rising and starting down the boulder-strewn peak. "I will return in an hour."

"Thank you, Fareed."

Awad sat down just below the top of the boulder. Far enough up on it so that he could see down the northern slope, but not so high as to silhouette himself once the sun rose above the eastern rim of the volcano.

"Fareed, wait," Awad said. "Do you have a cigarette? I left mine in my tent."

The cook turned around and came back up onto the boulder, sitting down once more. Reaching into his shirt pocket, he took out a pack of strong Turkish cigarettes and shook two out, handing one to Awad.

He struck a wooden match on the surface of the rock, and it flared brightly. When the flame subsided, Fareed held it out to Awad first and then lit his own, as Awad turned his head upward, exhaling the rich smoke.

"In three days, we will not be allowed to smoke anything but the American cigarettes," Fareed complained.

"At least Hussein agreed to that, my friend. After Majdi and I told him everyone in America smokes them."

"You couldn't have told him they smoked a good Turkish blend?" the older man asked, taking a deep draw on the strong smoke and exhaling over his shoulder.

Awad laughed lightly, looking up at the night sky. A bright star directly above them and very near the moon seemed to flicker, growing brighter as the dawn of a new day approached. Awad thought it a good omen.

CHAPTER
NINETEEN:

Chyrel Koshinski was in her office in Homestead very early, well before the sun had even thought about rising. She liked to start her day early and often worked late into the night. This morning, she was up much earlier than usual.

Deuce had texted her late last night from his new office in the nation's capital. He had an assignment for her that involved moving the surveillance satellite they sometimes used. He said he'd email the location to her office and she could then move the satellite into geosynchronous orbit above a suspected terrorist training camp to begin observation.

With the satellite currently parked in space above the Gulf of Mexico, Chyrel knew it would take several hours to move it into position over whatever Middle Eastern country he wanted to look at with its sophisticated camera equipment.

In her tiny office, Chyrel booted up her desktop computer and waited. When the secure client server came up, she opened the email and was surprised that the target area Deuce emailed her was in Mexico, not the Middle East.

Shrugging, she pulled up a terrain map of the target area, with lines of longitude and latitude laid out on it. Jotting down the exact coordinates of the suspected camp, she opened the control panel for the satellite and entered the numbers from her pad.

The computer told her the satellite would be over the target in less than an hour, so she spent the time studying the geography, using both the terrain map and a satellite image from Google.

Though Google images are sometimes years out of date, she liked playing with them. Sometimes, the angle of the sun would show shadows and give her a better idea of what a place was like. Occasionally, she went to the street view to see regular people going about their day. Lately, she'd been zooming in on boat wakes she saw in the water, to look at people on their boats. This time, even though the Google image was overgrown with trees and shrubs, the shape was still unmistakable.

"Huh," she said aloud. "Hiding in a volcano?"

Referring to the terrain map, she saw that the mountain, called Vulcan de San Martin, was a long-dormant volcano about twenty or so miles inland and southeast of Veracruz. The concentric rings of the terrain map showed that it rose steeply from the barren plain to a fractured cone at just over a mile above sea level.

The cone itself appeared to be roughly circular, at just over a half mile wide. Looking back and forth from the terrain map to the Google image, she noticed that the western slope was carved with deep gouges, canyons with a vertical drop of several hundred feet in places. The southern and eastern slopes were heavily forested, and the north slope looked like a moonscape, mostly bare rocks and sand. Zooming in, she saw several areas with round depressions that she realized had been made centuries ago by cooling lava forming bubbles.

The rim of the crater was highest on the north side and lowest on the south. It looked like the jungle just spilled into the nearly flat area of the cone from the south side.

A ping from the satellite control panel let her know the orbiting spacecraft was in place. Knowing that Deuce wouldn't be in his office for at least a couple of hours, Chyrel switched the satellite's camera equipment on to have a look.

It was still full darkness, so the digital camera showed nothing but blackness. When Chyrel switched it to thermal imaging, what she saw startled her.

Near the center of the crater was a very large, very hot spot. Curious, she zoomed in and activated the sensory systems. The display on the side of the thermal image indicated the surface at the center of the twenty-foot-wide hot spot was over one hundred and fifty degrees. Moving the sensor just fifty feet away, she found that the surface temperature was a relatively cool seventy-two.

When Chyrel zoomed back out to show a five-mile square, she realized what the hot spot was. Molten lava below the surface was heating the ground.

At the same time she realized this, she noticed about a dozen much smaller and cooler hot spots on the southern slope and a solitary one on the northern rim. She zoomed in on the tight cluster to the south. All but four were in groups of two and appeared to be people lying down. When one of them began to move, she was sure of it.

"Guess the reports are right," she said to herself.

"What reports?" a voice asked from her open door.

Chyrel looked up and smiled at Tony Jacobs, one of the field guys with the Caribbean Counterterrorism Command. A shaved-headed black guy with a muscular physique, he was by far the friendliest of the group of always-serious spec-ops spooks she worked with.

"Deuce has me looking at a volcano in Mexico where reports have said a terrorist cell had set up a training camp."

Tony came around Chyrel's desk and bent over to look at the image on her screen. Most of the team members had security clearances as high as, or higher than, her own. Tony was Deuce's right-hand man and had come with Deuce to work at Homeland Security from the Navy SEALs. They had a lot of history, and the boss trusted him completely.

"Sure looks like a group of people," he said. "Hey, look. That guy's moving."

As they watched, a solitary figure began weaving away from the group, moving to the north. Thermal imaging can't distinguish features, or even differentiate between a ninety-eight-degree rock and a person. All it measures is differences in heat, so a person against a cold background looks like a ghostly apparition.

"There's one more about a mile north of these," Chyrel said, zooming out. "And check this out."

"Whoa!" Tony exclaimed. "What the hell is that? A fire?"

"This whole area," she said, making a circular motion around the bright spot on the screen. "This is the volcano's crater. From what I've found out, it hasn't erupted in over two hundred years."

Tony laughed. "Looks like we might not even have to worry about these guys."

"Maybe, maybe not," Chyrel said. "I don't know squat about volcanoes. They might stay hot like that all the time."

"That guy's walking right past the hot spot," Tony said. "Follow him."

Chyrel worked the keyboard, zooming out until both the moving person and the one on the north rim were in view. As the one drew nearer, she zoomed in slightly. "Where this person is," Chyrel said, pointing to the stationary one, "is the highest part of the rim. A lookout, maybe?"

"And you think you're no good at sleuthing?" Tony said, mocking her. "The others are sleeping and that guy is on his way to relieve the sentry. I'd bet where that other guy is, it's a lot higher ground."

Pulling the terrain map back up, she pointed to a spot on the north rim, where the circles lay very close together, indicating a cliff. "That spot is a good hundred feet higher than the rest of the rim and nearly five hundred feet higher than the center of the crater. The elevation there is fifty-four hundred and ten feet above sea level."

"Good choice for an observation post," Tony said. "He can probably see all the approaches to the mountain from there."

Just then, the moving figure arrived at the solitary person's location, and Chyrel zoomed in a little more.

After a moment, the original lookout started to move away, but stopped and came back again. A sudden hot spot appeared briefly between them, and Chyrel quickly switched to digital imaging and zoomed in tight on the two, activating the record function. Two men appeared to be sitting together, a flickering light between them. The light disappeared and two small glowing spots became visible, then one of the spots suddenly brightened for a moment.

"They're smoking cigarettes," Chyrel said.

Tony chuckled. "Two on a match."

"Huh?"

"Never light two smokes on a single match," he explained. "A good sniper can identify you as a target when the match is struck, aim as the first guy lights up and fire when the second guy does. The second guy on a match is the dead man. Why's Deuce have you watching these clowns?"

"He didn't say, but I'm taking notes and recording everything. He's supposed to call at six."

"Can you play that back?" Tony asked, leaning in closer and going down on one knee. "In slow motion?"

"Sure," Charity replied and tapped a few keys.

She clicked the button to play at half speed. Initially, the image was distorted, as the camera had been zooming in when she'd started the recording. As the second man lit a cigarette, the first turned his face upward, the glow from the other man's match and the moon illuminating his face for a moment.

"Go back," Tony said. "Then go forward frame by frame."

"This is a high-speed camera, Tony. Frame by frame of just those three seconds is over a thousand frames."

"Can you go ten frames at a time?"

Chyrel backed up the recording, then moved it forward as instructed.

"Stop," Tony said. "Now go one frame at a time."

After clicking a few more frames, Tony stopped her again. "Look there," he said. "That's a Russian-made Bizon SMG machine pistol on his lap."

"And a pretty decent image for facial recognition."

"A lot of Afghan fighters use those weapons. The Russians left a bunch behind when they pulled out. Pretty good indication that you found a possible terrorist cell, Chyrel."

"I'll send the facial image to a friend at Langley," she said, fingers flying on the keyboard. "And flag it high priority. I should be able to identify at least this one guy before Deuce calls."

"Think he'll send one of the teams down there?"

"Into Mexico? I doubt it. Probably just follow them and bust them if they cross into the US."

"If the volcano doesn't explode and take them out first," Tony said with a grin.

Tony exited her office then, leaving Chyrel to monitor the terrorists. The two on the north rim split up, but the one leaving didn't return to the group. Instead he crossed the crater and started a fire, just inside the south rim.

Chyrel zoomed in tight on the man as he moved around the fire, hoping he would look up at some point. By the fire's light, she could tell he was the group's cook as he went about preparing their meal, shielded on three sides by giant boulders. Pinpointing the spot of the fire, she made a note of its precise location, as well as those of the camp and lookout positions. Finally, the cook stretched out on a rock near the cook fire, and she was able to get a fair image of his face by the flickering firelight. She sent that off to her friend as well.

While she watched, the others at the camp began to stir and, one by one, they made their way to the fire. In less than an hour, Chyrel received an email from her FBI contact at Langley. She read over the two files that were attached and then saved them, to send to Deuce when he called.

One of the men broke away from the others at the campfire and headed toward the high escarpment of the lookout post. The sun hadn't yet made its way into the crater, but there was enough light now that she had no trouble seeing all of them with the digital camera.

The rest of the group then arranged themselves in a curved line, and it looked like they were all pointing at a large rock. She suddenly realized they weren't pointing, but were aiming guns, as she saw sparks fly off the boulder.

Chyrel quickly recognized where the huge, round boulder was. She switched back to the thermal imaging camera, and the sight actually made her laugh.

"Better not mess with Mother Nature, guys," she said as the group of men fired automatic weapons at the dome-shaped hot spot in the center of the volcano crater. Each bullet made a white-hot line from the shooters to the large glowing rock, then ricocheted off to the left or right.

Minutes later, the vid-com icon at the bottom of her screen flashed and she opened it. Deuce's face appeared, sitting at a desk in a large black leather chair, dark paneling behind him.

"Hey, Boss," Chyrel said. "The seat of government looks good on you. But that bare wall needs a woman's touch. Julie hasn't been there yet, huh?"

"She's coming by for lunch," Deuce said from his new office in Quantico. "Find anything interesting yet?"

"Yeah, but it's one of those good news, bad news kinda things."

"I could use some good news, but give me the bad news first," Deuce said.

"Bad news is, and Tony pretty much confirms it, there's a terrorist cell of fifteen people, currently training in the crater of a volcano in Mexico."

The look on Deuce's face spoke volumes. He already knew this. "What's the good news?"

"The volcano might erupt any minute and kill them all."

Deuce's eyebrows shot up. "What?"

"I don't know anything about volcanology," she said, patching the thermal feed to his computer. "But the thermal imaging camera shows a really hot area inside the crater, and those idiots are shooting at it. Real hot. Like over one fifty. But an eruption is really just wishful thinking. The real good news is, I've already IDed two of them."

"Why does this strike me as ironic?" Deuce said with a wide grin.

"Yeah. And I have the best seat in the house if they blow the mountain up."

"Good work," Deuce said. "Shoot what you have to me. How did Tony confirm the people are terrorists and not a Boy Scout troop playing with automatic weapons?"

Chyrel clicked a few keys, and the image appeared of the first man she identified. "He didn't see the shooting part. I'll have to get him back in here to see it, though. He'll get a kick out of that. Anyway, this is Awad Qureshi, age twenty-three. Tony says the weapon in his lap is a Russian Bizon SMG. Qureshi is an Afghan student attending college here in the States, studying physics. Originally from the Arma Mountains region of Afghanistan. I ran a quick background check, and he hasn't been on campus for two weeks."

"Who's the other guy you identified?"

Chyrel made a few more keystrokes and the other man's face appeared. "This is Fareed Basara, also an Afghan national, but from a nomadic tribe. He's been seen on the battlefield in northern Afghanistan and was reported entering Guatemala three weeks ago."

"Good work, Chyrel," Deuce said. "This is a highly sensitive situation. But is there any way you can have someone knowledgeable in volcanoes look at that thermal image and tell you if it's normal or if the thing's really about to blow?"

"Sure, Boss. I know a guy studying volcanology in Hawaii. He might even still be up. It's like midnight in Hawaii right now."

"Let me know right away if you learn anything more."

The screen went blank, and Chyrel went back to the thermal image. The sun was high enough now that she was able to add digital imaging to the thermal scan.

Zooming in to isolate the hot spot and keep the shooters out of the frame, she pinpointed several spots in a circle around the large boulder, each showing up as a number on the image corresponding with a temperature readout for that spot on the sidebar. Then she took temperature measurements of several spots within the hot spot, though they only differed by a few degrees, cooling toward the edges.

Taking a screenshot of the whole digital and thermal image, she attached it to an email and sent it to her friend in Hawaii.

His response was almost immediate and said that the large boulder was actually the dome of a fumarole that could very well collapse and spew lava into the crater within a matter of days. Chyrel forwarded the information to Deuce.

CHAPTER TWENTY:

Halfway to Alvarado, the winds had shifted, just as Charity had known they would. Her speed had slowed to just seven knots, as *Dancer* sailed a broad reach.

Approaching the harbor as the sun was setting, she doubted she'd be able to rent a vehicle until morning. But she had found a marina that had parking close to the slips. She'd called to see if one of the slips near the parking lot was available.

The marina operator had said they had plenty of slips available and she could take any of the center ones, close to the parking lot. He'd asked if she needed to clear customs, and she'd told him she'd already done so in Progresso and gave the man her alias name and the boat's name.

Half an hour later, as the sun disappeared over the hills to the west, Charity had the boat tied up, connected to both shore power and water. She hadn't started the engine until she was approaching the marina, so she hadn't used more than a gallon of fuel, including leaving Progresso.

The marina operator was disappointed that she wouldn't need fuel, but when he saw that she'd already connected water and electricity, he brightened up.

"How long will you be staying, Señorita?" the weathered old man asked.

"Two days," Charity replied. "Maybe three. Do you know anywhere I can rent a car or a truck? I have friends in La Tinaja."

"I have a truck," he said. "I let cruisers use it from time to time."

"You do?" Charity asked, more upbeat.

"Yes, but two men rented it earlier today. They promised to have it back by midnight, so you may rent it in the morning."

Morning? Charity thought. There had to be a way to get the keys tonight, without raising suspicion.

"I was hoping to leave very early," she said. "Do you know of a car rental place that is open before sunrise, perhaps?"

The old man thought for a moment. She knew he wouldn't willingly give up a cash customer to a real car rental company if he could avoid it.

He snapped his fingers and grinned, showing half his teeth missing. "Not early, *señorita*. But, old Pedro? He has an idea. The men who rented my truck will drop the keys in a box by my office. I will leave a note there for them to park it here near your boat. I have an extra key for it and will bring it to you now, so they will not have to wake you."

"Thank you, Pedro. That is very gracious. Should I pay the rental fee now?"

"Or later, *señorita*. When I bring you the key."

"How much?" She knew there would be some bargaining, but the price he asked was so ridiculously low, she agreed to it and paid him on the spot, along with a deposit for water and electric and three days' slip rental.

Five minutes later, Pedro returned and gave her a single key on a large carved wooden key chain. "It is just an old flatbed truck, *señorita*. Mostly blue, but living on the coast, it is also mostly rusty. But the engine? She is good. You will not be stranded on the road."

Charity thanked him, and after he left, she went back aboard to eat dinner and shower two days' worth of salt from her skin. She was tired, but still wanted to leave and get up to the volcano tonight.

She'd studied the satellite images and found a winding rutted road over rock and sand that ended near the northern base of the mountain. Two miles before its end, the road dipped into an arroyo and switchbacked around a boulder field. She could park in the arroyo and go the rest of the way on foot. At nearly three miles from the mountain, she doubted she'd be observed, and she planned to wear night vision goggles and drive the last couple of miles in total darkness.

After showering, Charity dressed in rugged black cargo pants and a black long-sleeved shirt, also with cargo pockets. She took her hammock and a plain black ball cap from the closet and went up on deck.

Seeing nobody, she hung the hammock below the boom. Under the port bench, she retrieved her Colt and, pulling the cap over her face, settled in for a short nap.

Hopefully, the sound of the truck would wake her. But, just in case, she set the alarm function on her watch for one o'clock, local time. That would give her plenty of time to get there. With the Colt at her side, Charity fell asleep.

Shortly after midnight, the chugging exhaust of the marina operator's truck woke her. From under the hat, she watched as two men got out and staggered toward the marina office before heading further down the dock.

When the men were out of sight, Charity rose from the hammock and went down to the cabin to get her equipment. Everything she'd need, she'd already put into her backpack, except the rifle. Stored in the black case, she hoped it would be inconspicuous enough.

Before locking up, she checked the laptop for messages. There was a long one, with several attachments. Reading the message and studying the images attached, she had a sudden but fleeting feeling of dread.

The volcano could erupt at any minute? Charity thought.

Pushing the thought from her mind, she studied the terrain map. Someone had pinpointed several places with corresponding geographical coordinates, indicating the locations of the terrorist camp, the sentry, and the cook fire. Another spot was identified as the volcano's fumarole dome, with a current surface temperature of one hundred and fifty degrees.

The sentry location was a problem. Deuce himself had helped teach her the finer points of sniping. Even McDermitt had given her some pointers, as well as Donnie Hinkle, the Australian sniper on the team. Lastly, the young Marine she'd spent time with and who was killed a few months ago, had said the same thing when she was in a lighthouse with him in Key West.

"Snipers need to command the high ground," they'd all advised her.

She'd planned on using the same high cliff for her hide that the terrorists had set up as their lookout post. This meant she'd first have to kill whoever was there. Which meant she needed to know their schedule for relieving one another.

She wrote a quick response, asking for any information on how often they changed sentries and at what times. But, since she needed to get moving now, she asked that her message be sent to Deuce at once. She'd be able to access the email server on her encrypted sat-phone.

Putting on her web belt with several equipment pouches and canteens of water, Charity holstered the Colt and put two loaded magazines in one of the pockets. She tossed a two-hundred-foot coil of black nylon mountaineering rope over her shoulder and went back up on the deck. Kneeling in the cockpit, she watched the other boats and the parking lot for a couple of minutes.

Satisfied that nobody was watching, she rose. Picking up the backpack in one hand and the rifle case in the other, she hurried to the truck and tossed them in the open passenger-side window.

Going around to the other side, she opened the door as quietly as she could and climbed in. Sitting low in the seat, Charity looked around the parking lot again before starting the truck and driving out of the marina.

She'd already programmed the GPS on her sat-phone for the fastest route to the dirt road leading to the north slope of the volcano. Following the directions of the GPS, Charity was soon on the outskirts of town, heading east on Mexico Highway 180.

Once she was in the rural countryside, she found a wide shoulder and pulled over. From her backpack, she took out a white Mexican-style blouse and unbuttoned her cargo shirt halfway, tucking the lapels inside. Then she put the white blouse on over it. There were toll booths on the road, and she hoped to be able to pass herself off as a simple farming woman, heading back to the farm.

Back on the road, she made it past the toll booths without incident, and thirty minutes later, in the tiny town of Tula, she turned left onto Avenida Cesareo Carvajal, the dirt road that wound along the coast to the volcano.

Ninety minutes and twenty bone-jarring miles later, Charity reached the arroyo, where she would leave the truck. She hadn't seen another vehicle since turning off the main road and had driven the entire length of the dirt road with the lights off, wearing night vision goggles.

Pedro had been right—the truck was old and rusted, but the engine chugged its way up and down the ravines with ease, though the suspension could probably use some work.

Charity quickly turned the truck around and backed it behind a large boulder where the arroyo was widest, the transmission whining loudly in reverse. After she shut the engine off, the only sound she could hear was the ticking of the exhaust as it cooled in the night air.

Climbing out of the truck, she shed the white blouse and tossed it onto the seat of the truck, then buttoned her cargo shirt to the neck. She quickly pulled her hair back, secured it with a band, and put her cap on. Looking around, she saw nothing but rocks and fine powdery sand. Off to the east, clouds were building, and there was an occasional flash of lightning.

A thunderstorm would be good, Charity thought.

She pulled her backpack on, opened the rifle case and slung the rifle over her shoulder. Together, they weighed nearly forty pounds, but she'd hiked with heavier packs before. Just not at a mile above sea level. She'd have to be careful to not overexert herself. Before leaving the truck, she checked the email server to see if there had been a reply to her query.

There was one from Deuce personally, telling her the sentries appeared to change in two-hour shifts, close to the even hours. The cell members ate breakfast in the crater before sunrise and conducted live fire practice until noon. He added at the end that most of the terrorists had been seen in satellite images to be smoking cigarettes and several more had been identified.

All those identified were known terrorists, with the exception of the college student. All were to be considered enemy combatants, and she was free to engage at will. Again, he wished her Godspeed in her mission.

Charity checked the time. It was three o'clock. The sentry's position was three miles away, the last mile being an ascent from two thousand feet to over five thousand feet along a treacherous hiking trail. Traversing the rough terrain on foot would take her more than two hours. She would get there with maybe an hour before the sentries changed and two hours before dawn.

She would wait in hiding until the sentries changed at dawn. That would allow her two hours to eliminate the lookout, identify the leader, and kill him.

With single-minded determination, Charity stepped away from the truck and trudged steadily up the road and out of the arroyo. Even if they had night vision, which she doubted, the distance made it nearly impossible to make anything out. The mountain appeared against the star-filled background, black and foreboding, as if it could explode at any minute.

CHAPTER TWENTY-ONE:

Awad didn't sleep well. After being awakened by a bad dream, he couldn't get back to sleep. In his dream, some kind of predatory black cat was stalking him. Invisible in the darkness, the cat spat laser-like projectiles at him from far away. When the great cat breathed fire at him, he awoke, shaking.

Checking his watch, Awad saw that it was still two hours until sunrise. In the distance, he could hear the now-familiar rumbling of thunder, only closer this time.

Awad was ready to leave this place. Predatory fire-breathing animals and heavy rainstorms were things he wasn't accustomed to. Neither in his home-land, nor where he went to school in California. They'd been here for the better part of three weeks now, and he was having serious doubts about going through with the mission.

Having a valid American visa, he could easily slip away from this group in Reynosa and cross the border legally, just as he'd done in Arizona, when entering Mexico. Rolling out his mat, Awad prayed for the next hour, asking Allah to guide him in his decision.

When he finally left his tent, backpack flung over one shoulder, he saw Majdi was again on watch in the camp and walked toward him.

"Less than two days until we leave this place," Karim said quietly, seeing Awad approach.

"I will be glad to be gone," Awad replied in a whisper, sitting down next to the man. "I did not sleep well last night. I dreamed of a black jungle cat stalking me and spitting fire."

"A black jungle cat? There is an occasional mountain lion here, but they are sandy colored. The black ones live much further to the south."

"Nevertheless, it was a frightening dream. Who is on watch on the mountain?"

"Faud just relieved me," Karim replied. "Fareed will take his morning meal and relieve him, when we finish eating. He should be leaving to start the cook fire very soon."

"Do you think we are ready?" the younger man asked.

Karim thought it over a moment. "Yes, I do. The border is very porous and easily crossed. Our target is unprepared. The infidels have grown lax in the five years since our brothers' glorious triumph in New York. The infidels have no stomach for a long fight."

A stirring caught their attention, and they both turned toward the sound. Fareed exited the tent he shared with Faud and walked toward them.

"*As-salamu alaykum*," Fareed whispered, kneeling next to Awad.

"*Wa-Alaikum-Salaam*, Fareed," Awad replied. "Do you need help this morning?"

"Yes, please," the cook replied. "Faud tossed and turned all night. I will take both our meals up to the post early, so he might get some rest before target practice."

"What about yourself?" Awad asked.

"I will get plenty of rest in paradise when this is over. Besides, my tribe is known for sleeping very little."

A flash of lightning from the far side of the mountain got all three men's attention, and they turned. The loud crack of thunder split the air a few seconds later.

"It will rain this morning," Karim said. "With this lightning, you will be wise to stay lower than the surrounding rocks."

Fareed looked at Majdi for a moment, thinking the man was testing his resolve. "I cannot see through rock," Fareed replied, giving the answer he thought Hussein's third-in-command wanted to hear. "I will be alert and watching as always."

Fareed and Awad stood, and then started up the familiar path to the volcano's crater. Once they were out of earshot, Awad whispered, "I know you said that only for Karim's sake. But he is right. Lightning will strike the highest object. Nobody ever drives by this mountain at night, and very few during the day. Do what is safe. We cannot afford to lose a man five days before we strike."

The two walked in silence and reached the cook area in ten minutes. Fareed began to build the fire and Awad, familiar with his habits, brought water from one of the cans, stored out of sight. Using a ladle, he measured the correct amount of water into the large pot suspended over the now-flickering fire.

Fifteen minutes later, when the stew was finished, Fareed put some in two containers and stored them in his backpack. He then removed the large pot from the fire and placed it on a rock to cool.

"I will take Faud his meal and eat my own up there," Fareed said, jerking his head toward the high cliff, while shouldering his pack.

"Be careful," Awad said, sitting down on a rock to wait for the others. "Karim has not been wrong about the weather yet. If he said it is going to rain, it will."

The older man nodded. "I will see you on the shooting range in three hours."

Awad checked his watch, as yet another bolt of lightning crisscrossed the sky, cutting a jagged line in the blackness, the attending thunder echoing in the deep canyon.

It was still an hour until sunrise. Opening his backpack, he dug around until he found his cigarettes and shook one out, lighting the smoke from the red-hot ember of a twig from the cook fire.

As he squatted there, Awad stared into the dying flames and thought again about his dream. After a moment, as the first fat raindrop sizzled on a rock by the fire, he decided the omen in his dream must be the approaching storm.

Awad dug into his backpack once more. Finding what he was looking for, he took out a rolled-up waterproof poncho and pulled it on. Arranging the poncho around him, he pulled the hood over his head. He hoped Fareed and Faud had theirs with them, to at least shield themselves from the rain.

One by one, the other men began to arrive, and Awad took over Fareed's job of ladling out the spicy stew. Once everyone was there, he put some in his own bowl and sat down with Hussein, away from the others. As the heavens opened up and the rain began to fall heavily, Awad realized that even in this desolate place, the rain pouring down, he was at least alive and wanted to continue living.

"Today will be good training," Hussein said, bringing Awad back to the present. "We have no way of knowing what the weather will be like when we attack in San Antonio."

Awad only nodded. Just then, he decided he wasn't going to go through with it. He'd become enamored with the American lifestyle and wanted nothing more than to return to his studies and nightly parties.

Hussein ate quickly, urging the others to do so as well. "Let us take advantage of this weather and ready ourselves to fire the weapons in the rain!" he shouted, putting his bowl away in his backpack.

"Yes!" Awad shouted to the four men in his group, overcompensating for his doubts. "Eat quickly and move to the firing range. Shooting while it is still dark and in bad weather can only make us better."

Within minutes, the men were arranged around the giant round rock that they'd been shooting at for two weeks. Hussein was at one end of the semicircle and Awad at the other. The rain was falling lighter now, the short-lived storm moving away to the west. By the time the men removed their machine pistols and stood ready, guns hanging low at their sides, the rain had completely stopped.

Suddenly, Hussein raised his weapon and yelled, "Open fire!"

The sound of thirteen guns, all firing short bursts, nearly drowned out the thunderclap that rolled across the rim of the crater to the north. Had any of them been paying attention, they might have realized the booming thunderclap wasn't preceded by the usual flash of lightning. Or that the rock they were shooting at had grown more than five feet in width and a foot taller.

CHAPTER
TWENTY-TWO:

When the rain started falling in earnest, Charity began to move faster. The large boulder that was her objective was almost directly above her head. The goat path she was on continued at an angle to a gap between two large rocks, east of there.

Small rocks on the steep slope became dislodged by the water flow, adding to the sounds that masked her movement. The tiny gap meant she would have to get down on her hands and knees to get through to the inside of the crater.

Working quickly, the rain soaking her clothes now, she removed her backpack and slung the rifle over her head and shoulder, so it rested on her back. Through the gap, she could see a flickering light, bouncing off the rocks on the far side of the crater.

Charity drew her Colt and began moving cautiously through the opening, knowing it would be an ideal place for a booby trap. She probed the sand at an angle with a large Ka-Bar fighting knife, looking for an IED or trip wire, as she moved her pack forward inch-by-inch. After a few minutes, she reached the far side.

Slowly scanning the interior of the crater through the night vision goggles, she was able to make out a good bit of detail. The moon was halfway to the western horizon and had not yet been obscured by the growing storm.

To her right, she heard two clicking sounds and froze. The sound was familiar, almost like the sound a semiautomatic handgun makes when chambering a round. The ground in front of her flared into full brightness, allowing her to see the rocks ahead of her in great detail.

Realizing the sound wasn't a gun, but a cigarette lighter, she again studied the terrain below. This would be an ideal hiding place to wait for the sentry to change. Checking her watch, she saw that she'd made much better time than she'd thought she would. Sunrise, and the changing of the watch, was ninety minutes away.

A few minutes passed as Charity lay flat on her belly in the narrow confines of the rocks, shielded from the onslaught of the steadily falling rain. Across the crater, where the cook fire was hidden behind mountainous boulders, a man came into the clearing.

As the man walked across the nearly flat valley, she realized the sentry to her right was going to be relieved early. She lost him a couple of times, the gray-green image created by the night vision growing faint, as the storm clouds moved west, blocking the stars and moon.

Reaching into her pack with her left hand, Charity found the case containing her SPi T60 thermal monocular and switched it on to better track the man's progression across the crater. What she saw startled her for a moment.

Near the center of the crater was a huge glowing spot, much brighter than anything else. Remembering what the message had said, she knew it was the spout of the volcano.

What was it Deuce called it? Charity thought. *A fumarole?* It was huge, whatever it was. Rising above the crater floor at least ten feet, it had a base nearly thirty feet across.

As the man neared the fumarole, he stopped for a moment, as the wall of rain reached him. He appeared to squat down, and when he rose again, his temperature signature dropped. Charity set the monocular aside and switched back to the night vision scope. The man was now wearing a rain poncho.

As she heard the flick of the lighter again, with the brightening of the area directly in front of her, a plan quickly formulated in her mind. Ahead and to her left, just a few feet away, was another large boulder. The sentry to her right was probably expecting the early relief and a hot meal. He was also temporarily blinded from lighting another cigarette.

Those things will kill you, Charity thought sadistically as she quickly but quietly shed her gear and scurried forward around the rock to her left.

Charity stayed low, moving quietly down the hillside away from the sentry. Finally, she looked over a jagged volcanic outcropping and could see him easily by the light of his cigarette.

Glancing down, she saw that the other man was only a hundred feet away and would have to pass right in front of her, invisible to the man above.

With the rain dripping from the brim of her cap, Charity slowly drew the large Ka-Bar fighting knife from its sheath on her web belt, then pressed herself back into a deep crevice, waiting.

She didn't have to wait long. A few minutes later, the man walked slowly up the trail toward her position. Unsure of his footing in the darkness, he kept his head down. He had the hood of his poncho up over his head, so his peripheral vision was limited as well. A large bulge under the poncho told Charity that he was wearing a backpack under it. She didn't see any tell-tale bulge of a rifle, but he could easily have a sidearm concealed under the poncho.

As the man stepped directly in front of Charity, her right hand shot out, covering his mouth and yanking him back against her chest. Standing on her toes, she used his backpack for leverage and hauled the man's head back, exposing his neck. Panicking, he flailed his arms under the poncho, useless to defend himself. The knife came quickly across his throat, severing both artery and windpipe.

There was no need of a second thrust. The man would die in just a few seconds, and he was unable to make a sound. Charity pushed him forward as she slid the knife back into its sheath. He went down to his knees, hands reaching in vain for his neck, but only succeeded in getting tangled in the loose-fitting poncho. Charity stepped out and kicked the man in the back, sending him sprawling in the dirt.

"Karim! Is that you? Did you fall?" she heard a voice shout in Arabic above her.

In a guttural baritone, Charity moaned in perfect Arabic, "Yes! Help me!"

Charity pressed herself back into the crevice and waited, drawing her knife once more. In seconds, the other man came stumbling down the trail, going straight to the dead man in front of her. As he knelt over his fallen comrade, Charity quickly and silently stepped forward with her left foot and kicked the man hard between the legs with her right, connecting solidly.

He grunted hard, falling into a fetal position on his side, both hands holding his groin. Charity was on him in an instant. Rolling the man onto his back, she straddled his waist, clamping his hands and torso between her thighs like a vise.

The man opened his eyes and looked up at her, startled by the sight of her goggles. When he opened his mouth to scream, she thrust the blade of the knife deep between his ribs, yanking the handle left and right. He gasped, but made no other sound as he struggled in vain against her weight. A few seconds passed, Charity leaning hard against the knife's handle. Then the man's body went limp.

Rising, slowly, she pulled the Ka-Bar from his chest with a sucking noise. She lifted the man's poncho and wiped the blade off on his shirt before sliding it back into its sheath again.

Now it's only thirteen against one, she thought.

"I like my odds so far," Charity said to the two bodies lying in front of her.

She quickly went through their belongings. The one she'd just stabbed in the chest had had nothing on him but a pack of cigarettes and a lighter. In the other man's backpack, Charity found more cigarettes, two containers that were warm to the touch, and a machine pistol on a sling. She hung the weapon around her neck and picked up one of the containers. Pulling the lid off, she sniffed the contents.

Deciding she wasn't that hungry, Charity dropped both containers and hurried back up to the gap in the rocks, where she'd left her rifle and backpack. Feet first, she went back into the narrow opening. When her feet touched her backpack, she nudged it forward until she could reach it with her hand. Placing the pack in front of her, she rested the heavy rifle on it, flipping the bipod legs down and locking them in place.

Opening the rear cover on the scope, then reaching forward, she switched on the ATN optics and flipped its cover up. From her web belt pouches, she extracted three extra magazines. Two were loaded with ten of the massive fifty-caliber BMG match-grade boat tails. The third magazine was loaded with ten Raufoss armor-piercing incendiary rounds. She arranged them within easy reach, moving the one loaded with incendiaries to the far left side of the opening.

The rain seemed to be letting up as Charity looked through the scope toward the far side of the crater. The light from the cook fire behind the rocks illuminated the whole area on the far rim like it was midday. Several men could be seen coming out of the area behind the rocks where the fire was located.

As if a spigot had been turned off, the rain stopped. Charity scooted forward, craning her neck around the left side of the gap she was hiding in. Though it was still dark, the sky to the east was lighter now, and stars could be seen as the cloud cover moved quickly west.

Settling back down behind the scope, she could see a lot clearer now as the men formed a loose circle around the south and east sides of the fumarole. Each man had slung a machine pistol around his neck, just like the one she'd taken from the dead man. They held the weapons down at their sides, as if trying to hide them from someone.

As the men fumbled and arranged their weapons and ponchos, Charity moved the scope over each man, looking for her primary target. As she got to the last man, she recognized Hussein Seif al Din Asfour immediately from the pictures. The same man that had committed the terrible atrocities against his own people in Afghanistan.

The range was a little over four hundred yards with a declination angle of about thirty degrees. With the scope already zeroed at four hundred, she ran the declination calculation in her head. Below, inside the walls of the crater, there was almost no visible wind on the grass and shrubs, none that would deflect the massive half-inch-thick bullets, anyway.

As Charity studied the man's face, she wondered if there was anyone who would miss him. She tightened her fingertip against the trigger, aiming at a spot just below the man's Adam's apple. Slowly, her eyes closed behind the scope for a brief moment, opening that dormant part of her mind that contained all the hate, humiliation, and fury. When she opened them again, al Din Asfour's face transformed into that of the leader of the Taliban fighters who had held her captive and raped her repeatedly.

Charity slowed her breathing and relaxed her muscles. As she centered the crosshairs below his face, she allowed the reticle to move with the beat of her heart, falling squarely on his throat after each pulse.

Al Din Asfour moved, quickly raising his weapon and shouting something, but Charity moved the rifle with him, holding his neck steady in her sights. Squeezing the trigger a little more, she took the last of the slack out of it.

Timing the fall of the hammer with her own heartbeat, she heard the big rifle boom, just as the sound from the automatic weapons down below reached her ears.

Time seemed to slow as she watched al Din Asfour through the scope. His head suddenly jerked back. A greenish mist, as seen through the night optics, emanated from behind his head as the back of his skull literally vaporized.

Before anyone could react, Charity moved the sights to the next man in line and squeezed the trigger again. No longer waiting to see if it was a kill shot, she moved to the next man, killing him before the others even noticed. Suddenly, the terrorists realized what was happening and scattered toward the safety of the rocks around them, like cockroaches fleeing a bright light.

Charity scanned the area slowly, looking for another target. She'd already accomplished her assigned mission, but she was now playing by their rules. Which meant there *were* no rules, and no quarter would be given to anyone. She spotted a man who was crouched on the wrong side of a rock, looking up at the rim to the west. He was the sixth to die.

It became harder to find a target, the men crouched behind rocks and shrubs. But there were still nine men down there, and sooner or later, one would move. She held all the advantages. Cover, technology, greater range, and the vaunted high ground.

Charity's barrel swung left and right, when suddenly, a man made a dash toward the trail leading down to where she knew their camp was located. She sighted and squeezed, the big rifle roaring once more. Without waiting to see if he went down, she quickly went back to scanning the area for another target.

She found them all running toward the safety of the fumarole and returning fire wildly in her direction with the small machine pistols. The very best they could hope for was a one-in-a-million lucky shot. When they reached the rock they'd been shooting at, she saw one recoil away from its heat, leaving him exposed and in a sitting position. Charity put a bullet in his chest.

Seven men now hid behind the giant lava rock and seemed to be firing a lot more in her direction, having finally found the muzzle flash of the big Barrett rifle. But their weapons weren't even remotely accurate at this distance.

Charity grunted as she felt a tug at her right hip. At the same instant, she heard the crack and whine of a bullet ricocheting off the rock above her. It suddenly felt like someone had laid a red-hot fire poker against her ass.

Looking through the scope again, she saw another man stand, tossing his weapon away and raising his hands high above his head. When she shot him in the chest, the others rose and ran headlong for the safety of the crater's southern rim and their camp below it.

Charity dropped two more men as they ran. The other four managed to get in the tree line and disappear from sight. Calmly, trying to ignore the throbbing pain in her hip and the warm wetness on her outer thigh, she quickly removed the night optics attachment mounted in front of the scope. Setting it aside, Charity attached the thermal monocular to the Picatinny rail, locking it in place with her thumb. Settling behind the scope again, she looked through it into the far tree line. The range was eight hundred and twenty yards with a twenty-degree down angle. Charity ran the declination calculation in her head, as she adjusted the elevation knob.

The fumarole glowed white hot, halfway across the crater. In the distant tree line, she saw two hot spots, both very small, shielded by the coldness of solid rock. She placed the center reticle just below the first one and squeezed. One corner of her mouth went up in satisfaction as she watched the warm spray shoot up from the back of the man's head.

Inserting a second magazine, she looked through the scope and thermal monocular again, knowing that only three men were left. The other hot spot she'd seen was gone.

It was getting lighter now, but still dark in the forest eight hundred yards away. Charity patiently scanned the far rim of the crater. Night or day, the thermal optics worked the same. The only way to hide from it was to be behind something very dense or in front of something the same temperature as your body.

Charity wanted them all dead. Each one deserved a slow, cruel death, but dead was dead. If they didn't show themselves, she'd have to go after them. The magazine in the rifle was fully loaded with ten rounds. In close quarters, the machine pistol she'd taken from the dead man, or even her sidearm, would be preferable to trying to bring a thirty-pound sniper rifle to bear.

The throbbing in her backside had lessened somewhat, but that was going to slow her down. Knowing the three were in the opposite wood line, the idea of moving across the open terrain of the crater wasn't all that appealing either.

Glancing at the incendiary magazine, Charity had a thought. She looked up from the scope and scanned the crater floor and the high rim surrounding it. Her present location was a lot higher than any other part of the rim and a good four hundred feet above the crater floor, which seemed to slope slightly toward where the men had disappeared over the south rim. She could see tiny rivulets where rainwater flowed. They joined together and became the path down which the men had vanished.

I wonder, Charity thought as she scanned the trailhead at the opposite rim, by far the lowest point of the whole rim. Quickly, she dropped the magazine, inserted the Raufoss mag and ratcheted the bolt. The ejected round bounced off the rock to her right as a new round was chambered. One that could penetrate a half inch of steel and explode inside an armored vehicle.

"Wonder what these things will do against a volcano," Charity said aloud.

Studying the fumarole through the thermal optics, she dialed down the intensity until the great rock was barely glowing. Jagged white lines crisscrossing the rock became visible, like unmoving lightning bolts carved into the surface. They glowed brighter, because they were considerably hotter. On the northeast side, near the base, the thermal monocular showed a small jet of heat shooting up diagonally, swirling several feet out, before disappearing in the cool predawn air.

Charity aimed carefully at the spot where several lines came together and the jet of hot gas spewed out. She didn't know anything about volcanoes, but she knew that if there was a leak in her boat, making it bigger wasn't a good thing. Unless you wanted to sink the boat.

When she pulled the trigger, the white-hot flash of the incendiary round as it exploded was blindingly bright. When she looked again, the stream of gas was spewing a lot higher into the cool air. She fired again. And again.

The blinding flash of the third round was accompanied by a loud roar as the whole mountain seemed to vibrate.

This is stupid, Charity thought. Trying to set off a volcanic eruption when she was inside the crater was suicide. She fired a fourth round.

The whole mountain shook as the lava dome shattered and hot gases spewed into the air, hundreds of feet above the crater. Looking over the thermal scope, Charity witnessed a nightmare. Even with her tucked inside the narrow rock gap, the heat seared her skin. She pulled the backpack up for protection as the hot air inside the gap blew over her. Molten lava began to spill out of the fumarole, arcing away and splashing to the ground twenty feet away. The rock which had held the pressure of the gases in check for who knew how long was gone, shattered into millions of pieces.

Grabbing only the rope and leaving everything else, Charity scurried backwards out of the crack. The last thing she saw was red-hot lava, flowing freely like colored water. Filling the crater, it ignited everything it touched, flowing toward the low side.

CHAPTER
TWENTY-THREE:

W hat are you doing here so early?" Chyrel asked, entering the office.

"How could you go home?" Tony said, looking up from the computer screen. "This is like live sci-fi, and I'm the only one seeing it."

Pulling up another chair, Chyrel sat down next to the grinning black man. "I watched most of the night from my laptop. What'd I miss driving in?"

"I zoomed way out," Tony said. "About three hours ago, I saw a truck on a rutted road heading toward the volcano."

"I saw him on foot," Chyrel said.

"Yeah, he came the last three miles on foot, after parking the truck in a washout. He'd driven the truck without the lights on for quite a ways."

As the two watched, they saw the same thing happen that Chyrel had seen yesterday. "I watched these guys all day yesterday. Except for sunrise, they change lookouts every two hours." Pointing to the figure crossing the screen, she said, "That guy's relieving the other guy early, so he can go down and eat. Where's the guy from the truck?"

"Disappeared about twenty minutes ago," Tony said, watching the screen like a kid stares at a cartoon. He tapped a few keys, and the camera zoomed closer to the sentry's position.

"He went up here," Tony said, pointing. "Then disappeared into these rocks. Wait! There he is."

Over the next few minutes, the two watched as the man from the truck, who seemed to be dressed in dark clothes and a hat, made his way to a spot between the two sentries. Without warning, he apparently killed one, and the other came to investigate. The new guy then jumped on him and left him lying with the first sentry, apparently dead, as well. The man then went back to his hiding spot.

"Who is this guy?" Tony asked.

"I don't know, but I better get Deuce on this."

Chyrel picked up her phone and quickly called Deuce's secure line in Washington. "Get on the vid-com, Boss," she said, without waiting. "Something's happening on the volcano. A new guy just killed two of the terrorists."

"I'm in the office," Deuce replied. "Patch me in."

She ended the call and scooted Tony aside. In seconds, she set up a videoconference with Deuce's computer.

"Bring me up to speed," Deuce said over the vid-com.

Tony explained what he'd watched all night—the truck approaching, the man continuing on foot, and the quick killing of the sentry and his relief.

On the screen, the image dimmed. "Clouds are thickening," Chyrel said. "It started raining there a few minutes ago. Let me see if the thermal camera can penetrate it."

The thermal image was better, but lacked distinguishing characteristics because of the white-hot glow of the fumarole.

"What's the temperature of that thing now?" Deuce asked.

Pinpointing the center of the fumarole, Chyrel answered, "Over four hundred degrees." Clicking more keys, she added, "And it's grown sixty-three inches in diameter."

The thermal imaging dimmed to where only the fumarole was visible, but only barely.

"The storm is intensifying," Chyrel said. "But it's not very big, and it's moving quickly to the west. It should end in just a few minutes and clear up."

"Any idea who this guy is, Deuce?" Tony asked. "He one of ours?"

"No idea," Deuce said, but Chyrel could tell from his expression, even over the video feed, that he was lying. This troubled her. She'd never known the man to tell an untruth.

"It's clearing," Tony said. "And the sun's rising."

Chyrel switched back to the night optics camera and zoomed out to show the whole crater. The men at the fire had now formed a semicircle around the fumarole. Though she'd watched it happen yesterday, she was still amazed at their stupidity.

Just as the men began to open fire on the lava dome, the one on the left side went down, followed quickly by two more. Suddenly, the terrorists began firing wildly in all directions. Another went down and then a fifth when he tried to run to the south.

"It's a firefight!" Tony said. "The guy in the rocks is a sniper."

The remaining terrorists ran toward the fumarole, one colliding with it, then falling backwards. The sniper shot him as he struggled to get up.

"These clowns don't stand a chance," Tony said. "That guy has to be one of ours. He never looked up, so I couldn't get a picture for facial recognition."

At the side of the fumarole, they clearly saw a man toss his weapon away and step out into the open. The merciless sniper shot him where he stood, and the remaining men ran fast for the south side of the crater.

Two more terrorists were shot in the back, as the remaining three made it to the safety of the rocks at the edge of the jungle and took cover. One was suddenly yanked backwards, as if a spring had been released. The last two disappeared into the foliage.

"Dayum!" Tony exclaimed. "That crater's three-quarters of a mile across!"

Chyrel switched to thermal imaging and followed the two men through the jungle. They were headed to their camp. When they reached it, she zoomed out, to bring the sniper's hide back into the screen.

A laser-like line shot out from a spot on the north rim, appearing as a thin, white line of heat, striking the fumarole and erupting in a blinding flash of heat.

"Holy shit," Chyrel said. "He's shooting at the volcano!"

"Those are incendiary rounds!" Tony added, sitting forward.

One by one, three more shots struck the fumarole, when suddenly the whole screen went white.

"What the hell just happened?" Deuce asked.

Chyrel quickly zoomed further out, the widening hot spot expanding. "I think the volcano is erupting!" She glanced at the temperature sensor display, and her mouth fell agape. "Deuce, the temperature at the fumarole is over eighteen hundred degrees."

"Good God," Deuce said with a sigh. "She can't possibly survive that."

Chyrel switched to the regular camera and zoomed in. The sun was getting higher, and the glow from the spewing lava flow provided enough light that the night optics were no longer needed.

"Show me all the known locations," Deuce said.

Chyrel was frozen, mesmerized at the sight of the lava tumbling out of the fumarole and flowing like a red-hot river toward the gap in the rim.

"Chyrel!" Deuce snapped over the vid-com.

"Sorry, Boss," she replied and quickly pinpointed the camp, the sniper's hide and the cooking area.

As the three watched in horror, the lava swiftly flowed past the rim's gap, pouring freely down the southern slope, igniting and vaporizing everything in its path. The fleeing men didn't stand a chance.

"There!" Tony yelled, coming to his feet and pointing at the top of the screen. "Is that the sniper?"

Zooming in quickly, Chyrel found a solitary figure, dressed in black, scrambling down the north slope, in a straight downhill run.

"He's on rappel," Tony said. "Go, man! Get the hell out of there!"

The fleeing sniper must have reached the end of the rope and started moving along a trail to the northwest. Suddenly, the figure stopped and looked up into the sky. Chyrel quickly zoomed in tight on the sniper's face and gasped.

"That's Charity!" Tony exclaimed.

"Chyrel," Deuce said. "Stop recording now. Delete everything after you just zoomed in."

"Deuce! Charity's alive!" Chyrel said and it suddenly dawned on her what the man had earlier said, "*She* can't possibly survive that."

"You two are to forget what you just saw," Deuce ordered. "Is that understood?"

"Yes, sir," Tony replied, with a bit of a grin. "Forget what?"

"Chyrel?" Deuce asked.

Her hands danced across the keyboard, zooming the camera out to a five-mile radius and stopping the record function. Suddenly, the whole mountain seemed to explode, throwing rocks and ash in all directions.

Chyrel's hand flew to her mouth, and Tony's sardonic grin disappeared.

EPILOGUE

 early a week later, Deuce and Chyrel videoconferenced, having both tried and failed to find out more, or piece together Charity's movements to get to the volcano. All they could come up with was when Tony had zoomed out and noticed the truck driving on the rutted dirt road with its lights out. They had no way of knowing how she had arrived in Mexico, or where. And Stockwell wasn't giving up anything. Further, he'd ordered the deletion of the entire video file.

"She had to have flown," Chyrel said.

"That Huey just doesn't have the range," Deuce replied over the encrypted videoconference call. "Besides, that'd be too conspicuous."

"An airliner's out. Too much chance of being spotted on the security cameras."

"She had to get there in a boat of some kind," Deuce said, thinking. "I'd like to think she'd survived the eruption. But, without knowing where and how she exfiltrated, there's just no way to know for sure."

"Until Travis sends her on another mission."

"If so, he'll have to bring me into the loop," Deuce said. "Until then, the only ones who know it was her at the volcano are me, you, and Tony. As much as I hate it, we've been ordered by the secretary to continue the lie that she stole the chopper."

"And if Travis doesn't send her on another mission?"

"Then we'll have to assume she was killed. It'll be months, maybe years, before the Mexican authorities can get in there to see the devastation firsthand."

"She kicked ass, though. Didn't she?"

Deuce smiled slightly. In just the two weeks since he'd taken the job in DC, Chyrel thought years had been added to his face.

"Yeah," Deuce replied. "She most definitely kicked some major ass."

Meanwhile, Travis Stockwell was living up to the illusion of a retired public servant, drinking and carousing up and down the middle and lower Florida Keys. Jesse McDermitt was barely taking out a charter a week, so he had plenty of free time.

While Deuce was in DC, trying to figure things out, Travis and McDermitt were on McDermitt's boat, ten miles south of the Keys. It was only the second charter since the rescue and takedown of the Haitian gang in the Ten Thousand Islands, two weeks ago.

The first actual charter that Travis went out on as first mate had been only a few days after the rescue mission.

A group of veterans, some disabled, from a town halfway up the Florida coast, had arranged that charter weeks before. They were with a nonprofit organization that built and remodeled homes for deserving vets. Most were members of a veterans' organization called Space Coast Paratroopers, though not all the volunteers were Army jumpers. Some of the volunteers had already received a newly remodeled house and now volunteered for the Homes for Warriors Project every day they could.

After that one, McDermitt canceled the next two, ostensibly to give Travis time to find a place to live. But the real reason was so McDermitt could spend some time with his family.

Today's charter was a group of tourists from Topeka, Kansas. They'd been fishing and drinking all day. McDermitt's daughter had come along to help show Travis what the actual duties of a first mate were. As near as he could tell, they were to keep the tourists happy, drinking, and catching fish.

Travis wasn't as charming as McDermitt's daughter, but he was able to build a rapport with the men in the charter and was soon laughing with them, baiting hooks, and handing out beers.

The charter customers were lounging in the cockpit below, drinking and already exaggerating about the fish they'd caught, as *Gaspar's Revenge* motored toward the town of Marathon.

Travis, McDermitt, and his daughter, Kim, were all on the bridge, off limits to charter customers, enjoying the daily dance the sun played with the water as it slowly sank toward the far western horizon.

Travis looked down at the Midwesterners and grinned. "You call this work? I feel like I'm robbing you of the two hundred."

"Be more than glad to not pay you," McDermitt said with a kind of lopsided grin that Travis had quickly learned meant he was sedately content.

"Oh no," Travis replied. "I'll need that money to wine and dine a tourist woman from Texas I met last night."

Both McDermitts laughed, and Travis noted it was a similar laugh. Then McDermitt turned suddenly serious. "Have you heard anything new on the search for Charity?"

Just then, Travis's cell phone rang. He picked it up and saw that it was an encrypted message from the bowels of the Pentagon. Clicking the icon, he read the short message.

Mission accomplished. Taking a couple of weeks in the Yucatan to recover. I need a new Barrett, optics, and a few other things. I'll call when ready.

Travis deleted the message and glanced up at McDermitt with a frown. Inside, he was very happy and relieved, though.

"No," Travis replied. "So far, nobody's told me anything about what's become of Charity Styles."

In the little Mexican port city of Progresso, Juan Ignacio had just finished bartering with a local restaurant owner. The man had ended up buying all sixty pounds of his day's catch for two thousand pesos.

Juan would never get rich at this rate, but he lived a simple life. His boat was his home. The cantina owner promised to return with his cart in less than an hour, so Juan went below to shower and dress for the evening.

Twenty minutes later, while hosing down the deck and waiting for the man to return his cart, Juan looked out to the jetty at the mouth of the harbor.

A beautiful sailboat was passing by close to the coast, its blue-and-white sails pulled in close as it sailed near the wind. Suddenly, the boat turned sharply through the wind and into the inlet. The sails crossed the deck cleanly fore and aft, and in perfect unison. But they were still hauled in tight.

When the wind caught the sails again, the boat heeled over sharply, coming into the harbor at a very fast rate of speed. Only a hundred meters from the pier, Juan saw the pretty woman that had been here nearly two weeks earlier.

As the sailboat grew nearer, Juan watched as the sails disappeared, drawn into their furlers. The sailboat slowed and Juan walked out to the foredeck, standing bare-chested, with his hands on his hips.

At the last second, the big sailboat turned. The engine reversed, bringing the boat to a stop with the cockpit just a few feet away from the pilings. Juan smiled as the beautiful woman stood up at the helm, smiling back.

"Do you have any fish to sell?" she asked.

"I am afraid not, *señorita*," Juan said. "I just sold my catch a few minutes ago."

"Did they ever find out what happened to that robber?"

"Yes, they did. I witnessed the fight myself. The police think it was a gang of drug smugglers."

"I'm sorry for leaving like that, Juan."

"I understand. Will you be staying long?"

"Depends on whether I can find a slip."

Juan looked at the empty berth next to his boat, where he had once had a second fishing boat. "I own both slips, *señorita*."

"Then I would say it depends on the fishing."

"And the dancing," Juan replied as Gabriela Ortiz backed her *Wind Dancer* into the slip.

THE END

If you'd like to receive my twice a month newsletter for specials, book recommendations, and updates on coming books, please sign up on my website:

WWW.WAYNESTINNETT.COM

THE CHARITY STYLES
CARIBBEAN THRILLER SERIES

Merciless Charity
Ruthless Charity (Summer, 2016)
Heartless Charity (Winter, 2017)

THE JESSE MCDERMITT
CARIBBEAN ADVENTURE SERIES

Fallen Out
Fallen Palm
Fallen Hunter
Fallen Pride
Fallen Mangrove
Fallen King
Fallen Honor
Fallen Tide
Fallen Angel
Fallen Hero (Fall, 2016)

The Gaspar's Revenge Ship's Store is now open. There you can purchase all kinds of swag related to my books.
WWW.GASPARS-REVENGE.COM

AFTERWORD

One of my favorite writers, Randy Wayne White, started a spinoff series to his fantastic Doc Ford novels a little over a year ago. His new series has a female main character, and he made it look easy and effortless. Believe me, it's anything but. Even writing in an omniscient third-person point of view, getting inside Charity's head wasn't easy. I hope I've done half as well as Randy.

I'd dreamed most of my life about being a novelist. Growing up on the east coast of Florida, I cut my teeth on the works of Ernest Hemingway and John D. MacDonald, then, as a young man, James W. Hall, Carl Hiaasen, and Randy Wayne White, among others. My writing style and characters are a direct reflection of the musings of these and many more great authors.

Made in the USA
Coppell, TX
05 February 2022

72964997R00122